Little White Lies

Margaret Fenton

Aakenbaaken & Kent

Little White Lies
2nd Edition

Copyright, 2022 by Margaret Fenton, all rights reserved.

No part of this book may be used or reproduced in any manner whatsoever without written permission except in the case of brief quotations for use in articles and reviews.

aakenbaakeneditor@gmail.com

This is a work of fiction. Names, characters, places and incidents are either the product of the author's imagination or are used fictitiously. Any resemblance of the fictional characters to actual persons living or dead is entirely coincidental.

ISBN: 978-1-958022-10-8

Dedication

For Becky Beavis
and all the other child welfare social workers
out there making a difference.

Chapter One

Bombingham. That's what everyone called my beloved city of Birmingham, Alabama, in the middle of the last century, when somewhere around fifty bombings happened between 1947 and 1965 during the civil rights movement. Few of the murders of our black citizens were ever solved. The name reared its ugly head again in 1998, when Eric Robert Rudolph decided to show how pro-life he was by bombing the New Woman/All Women Health Clinic here, killing Officer Robert "Sande" Sanderson and blinding and maiming nurse Emily Lyons. I was really hoping we wouldn't have to go through this again.

It was a Tuesday afternoon in mid-January and it was freezing. I'd been investigating child welfare for the Department of Human Services for close to a decade, and it never got easier. Today, most of my coworkers and I were huddled in the DHS office working on the endless amount of documentation that goes with being social worker and avoiding the frigid wind outside. The decrepit heater in the building struggled against the twenty-degree temperatures. I was writing a court report but having trouble concentrating. With the icy temperatures outside, I was more worried about LaReesa than ever.

LaReesa Jones was a thirteen-year-old friend of mine. I'd met her last September when she was flirting with men in the parking lot of a Dollar General instead of sitting in an eighth-grade classroom. I'd wrestled for weeks over whether or not I needed to open an official investigation on her and her family, and in the end decided against it. Then her grandmother suffered a stroke, her three young cousins came into foster care, and LaReesa disappeared.

I'd called in all sorts of favors in my search for her. I spent many weekends driving around hoping to catch a glimpse. I'd notified her school, talked to several of her friends, and interviewed her small cousins without any luck. I prayed she had somewhere warm to sleep and something to eat. Her grandmother passed away in November, and I didn't even know if she was aware of that. I had nightmares of her returning home to find an empty house.

I was focused again on the court report when the explosion happened. It sounded like a loud boom, with metal clanging at the same time. Like a trash truck had dropped a dumpster—ten feet away.

My coworkers' heads popped out of their cubicles in the room, like meerkats.

"Did you hear that?"

"What the hell?"

"That sounded like an explosion."

"Christ, that was loud."

Everyone drifted over to the windows on the west side of the building. My boss, Mac McAlister, wandered out of his office to see what was going on. Through the windows we could see a massive cloud of yellowish-white smoke rising to the sky. It appeared to be about fifteen blocks away. Too far away to be in the civil rights district, home of the previously-bombed Sixteenth Street Baptist Church and Kelly Ingram Park. I struggled to remember what was over there.

Sirens sounded in the distance, no doubt headed in that direction. My cell phone pinged and I checked it. My colleagues were doing the same. "Explosion at the office of Birmingham mayoral candidate Dr. Marcus Freedman", said the alert.

"Oh man, I hope he's okay," I muttered. Dr. Marcus Freedman was a progressive candidate. African-American and a professor of Political Science at the University of Alabama-Birmingham. He and my father, Christopher, had done some community work together in the past. He was running as a Democrat and was promoting things like better public transportation and schools. I didn't live in Birmingham proper, but if I did, I would have voted for him.

It dawned on me that if this bombing was even suspected to be a terrorist plot, the streets of downtown Birmingham were going to be closed—and soon. I scampered back to my cubicle and gathered my coat and briefcase. My cubicle-mate, Russell, shot me a curious look.

"I've got an appointment."

"Really? Claire, I could have sworn you said at lunch you were here for the rest of the day."

I leaned closer to him. "Look, if there's even the slightest hint this is a terrorist bombing, they're going to shut this city down, and fast."

"Oh shit, you are so right." He put on his coat and grabbed his satchel, too. "Bye."

We exited the building down the back stairs, saying goodbye in the parking lot again. I cranked my ancient white Honda Civic and headed home via the back roads, which were already getting crowded. I caught a glimpse of I-65 South at one point. It was already a parking lot. It should have taken me twenty minutes to get to my home in the Bluff Park neighborhood, but it took forty-five. My driveway was empty.

Grant Summerville and I had moved in together over Christmas. It wasn't like we ever actually sat down and talked about it, or mutually decided this was what we wanted. He was staying over more and more and it just made sense to let his lease go at the first of the year. He was an easy roommate. He did the dishes and kept the bathroom clean.

I put my coat and the briefcase down, and went to the bedroom to change clothes. Back in the living room I turned on the TV. The local ABC station had live coverage at the site of the bombing, the hulking black reporter speaking frantically. I gathered that they were still trying to get the fire extinguished before searching for any victims. He was stationed a couple of blocks away and couldn't really see much, and there was no word yet on how many were killed. I wondered how whoever had done this had built a bomb. After 9/11, I thought it was impossible to get large amounts of explosives.

I walked back to what had once been my office. Grant had kind of taken over this room and turned it into his computer room. My inherited roll-top desk still sat in one corner, but now trestle tables sat against three walls and held two laptops and three desktops that were quietly humming away, as well as boxes of various computer parts. I opened my briefcase and removed my laptop. DHS technically didn't allow us to bring work home, but also realistically understood that it would never get done if we didn't. As long as we were careful about privacy and security, Mac looked the other way.

I started the court report again and then had an idea. I retrieved my cell phone and called Kirk Mahoney. Kirk was a friend of mine who worked for the local newspaper.

"Hey, beautiful." He always said stuff like that, and I just ignored him.

"Hey, you at the bomb site?"

"As close as I can be. It's a mess here. What do you need?"

"The TV doesn't really have any news. I just wanted the scoop."

"No scoop so far. Everyone thinks Marcus Freedman was campaigning over in Eastlake Park, so there's hope he's alive. We'll see."

"Oh, good."

"What are you up to?"

"Just working at home."

"I gotta go. Police chief's about to give a statement. I'll call you later."

He was gone before I could say goodbye. My next phone call was a bit more difficult. My father answered after the first ring.

"Hey, Dad. You watching the news?"

"Isn't it horrible? Why would anyone want to kill Marcus? You know, I was at that office volunteering just two days ago. It could have been me."

"There's hope Marcus is alive, you know. They haven't found his…I mean, they haven't located him yet. Some people are saying he was over in Eastlake."

"I know, but--"

"I know. I hope he's okay. I can't imagine who would want to do this."

Two court reports and a progress report later, I curled up on the sofa and turned on the news again. Marcus had been found alive and was rattled by the bomb. They played his interview several times. He had no idea who might have done this but they were working with the police and the FBI to bring the person or people to justice. Early thoughts were it might be racially motivated. They'd found a body at the site, badly disfigured, and were waiting to release the identity. Of course, they'd have to identify him first.

I went to bed that night snuggled up against Grant. The horrific news of the day had really quite shaken me. I had trouble falling asleep and slept restlessly. Random body parts filled my dreams.

My cell phone rang at six in the morning. I wiped the sand from my eyes as I answered.

"Hello?'

"Good morning, Sunshine!"

"Ugh, Leah, how are you so cheerful at this hour?" Leah Knighton ran the night unit at work, supervising the team that handled all the calls that came in after hours.

"Hey, I'm about to get off work, so, you know. I've got a case for you. The night unit doesn't want to take it because it's time for them to go home. I called Mac, and he said it's yours."

"Terrific," I muttered.

"How soon can you get here? I'm leaving in an hour."

"I'll be there in forty." I slipped out of bed after a gentle kiss on Grant's shoulder, then showered quickly and threw on some warm clothes. It took a few minutes to de-ice and warm up my car, which brought on new worries about LaReesa.

I parked in the back lot and got to Leah's office just as she was packing up. She handed me a thin file.

"Got a call from a daycare worker. She has a baby, young

baby, eight months old. She said the father never came to pick her up yesterday. Baby's name is Madeline O'Dell. Maddie for short. She's tried calling the dad's cell phone all night, no answer. Dad is a Jason O'Dell. Daycare worker took Maddie home for the night and brought her back there this morning. Still no word from the dad, so she called us."

I opened the file as Leah talked. The kid had no prior record with us. That was good news, since she was just eight months old.

Leah continued. "Here's the strange thing. There's no one listed as an emergency contact. You know, people usually put a grandparent, or an ex-husband or ex-wife. He listed no one. The day care owner said her office should have noticed that and followed up on it."

"Yep. Dad having custody is a bit unusual, too. Less so these days, though. I'm going to head over there." I gathered my coat.

"Any word on LaReesa?"

"None so far."

"Good luck."

"Thanks, I need it."

Alice's Angels was a small place on the south side. It looked like it was once a house, converted to an office, then converted to a daycare. The front yard was now a fenced-in, rubber-paved playground, with a large jungle gym near the open front door. I parked in the street and made my way to the door.

The lobby was full of men. Men in police uniforms and suits. There was one woman, middle aged with pretty gray hair cut in a bob, dressed in a suit with an elegant scarf around her neck. I was wondering what it must be like to work in such a testosterone-fueled field when she spotted me. She approached me and asked, "Can I help you?"

I showed my ID. "I'm Claire Conover, from DHS. I'm here about Madeline O'Dell."

She showed her ID and handed me a business card. "I'm Deborah Holt. FBI. Come on in."

"I'm looking for Alice Ellington. She called us about a baby that hadn't been picked up last night."

She nodded to a sixty-something year old woman sitting in the corner, weeping quietly. Her brown hair, streaked with gray, formed a bun on the back of her head. Her eyes were swollen from crying. She cradled a small bundle in her arms, wrapped in a blanket and cooing.

"What's going on?" I asked Agent Holt.

"A guy was killed in the bombing yesterday."

"Yeah, I heard that on the news."

"His name was Jason O'Dell. That baby Ms. Ellington is holding is his daughter, Madeline."

Chapter Two

I stood in silence for a few minutes while that sunk in, then asked, "So her father's dead. Do we have any other next of kin that's been identified?"

"Not so far."

"And I guess this wasn't a terrorist bombing?"

"It's not looking that way. There's some indication that it may be race-related."

"Yeah, that's what they said on the news." I walked over to Alice, who was still crying and holding the bundle in the blanket. The blanket was fleece, printed with pastel colored butterflies on white background. Tucked into the folds I could see a caramel-colored face with a head full of black hair and big brown eyes. Her little mouth was working hard on a pacifier. I stroked her soft cheek and muttered, "Hi, Maddie." I turned to Alice. "Is she biracial?"

Alice stood up. Bowed up, really, as much as one can while holding an infant. "Yeah, so? What of it? She's beautiful."

"She is. It was just a question. No offense intended."

"Her daddy was white. I assume the mother is black. Will that make it harder to find her a family?"

"It shouldn't. Babies of any race are usually easy to place." What was going to be difficult were the legalities of the thing. By law, I had to search for her biological family first, and put her with them if they so desired. If they did not, then foster/adoption was the next step. The first step was to find her a place for tonight. I spoke to the police officer who had already taken her into protective custody, and he left with little Maddie after I made arrangements to meet them at the magistrate's office at Family Court.

Foster care is a multi-tiered system. I had a list of emergency foster parents who took in kids for a short period of time, usually until they were reunited with their families, hopefully. We also have long-term foster parents, who essentially raise kids who can't be returned to their families. Then there are adoptive foster parents who take in kids with the hope of someday adopting them. A lot depends on whether and when the birth family's rights are terminated. Throw into this mix a handful of social workers and lawyers and judges and it gets rather complicated. For now, I needed to get back to the office and on the phone. I voiced this to the room and Alice started crying again.

"We'll take good care of her, I promise. Does she have a carrier, or diapers, or anything?"

"No, just the blanket."

"Okay, no problem." I kept two car seats in the trunk of my car just in case. I don't think they were going to win any safety awards, but they would do. I set up the one for infants in my back seat and met the officer at Family Court to pick the baby up. When we finished at the magistrate's office, Maddie was sleeping peacefully.

She was wide awake and screaming by the time I got to my office. I couldn't blame her, really. She'd had a rough day. Russell was there when I walked in and immediately took her from me. "Look at this sweet snuggle pooh! What's your name, precious face?"

"Madeline. Maddie for short."

"Why are we so upset, huh?"

"Well, her father was murdered in the bombing yesterday, for starters. Have we got any diapers?"

"Seriously?"

"Yeah. Diapers?"

He shrugged. "Check the closet downstairs."

I made my way to the overnight unit, which was dark and quiet during the day. Rummaging around in a closet there revealed some white onesies and a stack of disposable diapers that were likely going to be too small. I'd have to make it work for now. I dropped the stuff off at my desk with Russell and went to update my boss.

Mac McAlister had been with this agency since before Adam met Eve, as he liked to remind us. I, for one, had never seen him rattled. This case was no different. He gave me some petty cash so I could get some diapers that fit and told me to let him know if I needed additional help. Russell agreed to watch Maddie while I shopped, and when I returned to the cubicle most of my unit was huddled around Russell and the baby, bickering over who was going to hold her next.

I found the latest 621 form, the list of available foster placements. I took it to an empty cubicle and started calling down the list. A half-hour later I had a hit. The Davidsons had agreed to take her. I went back to my cubicle and broke the bad news to Russell, who had clearly fallen deeply in love with a girl for a change.

I packed her into the car seat and took off for Hoover, the suburb south of town that was also technically where I lived. Jack and Julie Davidson were an older couple like most of my foster parents. They greeted me with smiles and a warm home. They kept a nursery set up permanently upstairs, and said they had plenty of clothes and diapers. We sat in the expansive living room as they passed Maddie back and forth and gushed over her.

"Look, I have to tell y'all something, and I need you to keep it to yourselves."

Mr. Davidson looked at me. "That sounds ominous."

"Yeah, well, see, the reason Maddie came into foster care is because of the bombing yesterday. Her father was the man killed. I have no idea who her mother is, or where she is, or anything. If the press get word of this and somehow found out where Maddie is—well, you know."

"We can handle it," Mrs. Davidson replied. "Poor, poor baby."

I bid my goodbyes and knew I was leaving Maddie in good hands. I stopped at home for a quick bite and headed back to work. My afternoon was spent doing the documentation for her file and her scheduled court hearing for Friday. Then my cell phone rang.

Kirk. I answered. "Hey."

"Hey yourself. So word is they've identified the body from yesterday and he had a young daughter. You wouldn't know anything about that, would you?"

"You know the deal. I can't talk about it."

"I know the deal but I'm not letting up."

"You never do."

"Is she with you?"

"Off the record?"

"Really?"

"Really."

"Fine."

"She's fine." I had a sudden thought. "Have any of Jason O'Dell's family come forward yet? To talk to the press or claim the body? I need to find them."

"Not that I've heard. They get first dibs on the kid, right?"

"Well, I wouldn't put it like that, but yeah."

"Let me make some calls."

"I'll do the same."

"Wanna meet for drinks and compare notes?"

"Sounds good. Someplace in Hoover, please."

"Do you like Thai food?"

"Sure."

We decided on Taste of Thailand and agreed to meet at five-thirty.

I found the FBI agent's card from this morning and called her cell. "Deborah Holt," she answered.

I identified myself. "Have any of baby Maddie's family come forward? Has anyone claimed Jason's body? I'm legally required to see if his family will take the baby first."

"I see. No one has contacted us so far. Have you called the police department or the coroner?"

"Those are my next calls."

"Good luck."

"Thanks."

Calls to the police department and the coroner's office revealed the same answer. There was nothing I could do now but sit back and wait.

I did a couple of quick home visits before going to meet Kirk. Taste of Thailand was in a strip mall, way in the back, and when I arrived Kirk had gotten us a quiet booth. He'd come straight from a work out and his spiky, black hair was still wet from the shower. He was drinking a beer, and a glass of wine waited at my place.

"Sauvignon Blanc, right?" he asked.

"I can't believe you remember what I drink."

"I remember a lot of things."

I had quick flashback to the kiss we had shared in my kitchen a few months ago, and felt myself blush. I pulled a notebook out of my bag and found a pen. "What can you tell me about Jason?"

"Well, he and Madeline had a two-bedroom apartment in Birmingham, in Southside, on Fourteenth Street. Right now, it's being guarded by the cops. I went to the office and charmed the secretary into showing me the lease. He's lived there two years, so before Maddie. He was a young guy, too, only twenty-two. I knocked on a few neighbors' doors but no one really knew him. Said he was pretty private. They don't remember a woman ever living there, or coming over, either, so no clue who the little one's mom might be." He handed me a sushi menu as the waitress approached. After a quick glance I ordered the vegetable sushi and Kirk got a Super Crunch.

"I need to go by his apartment and pick up some of the baby's stuff. I'll do that first thing tomorrow."

"Can I go with you?"

"If you stay out of trouble."

"Aw, that's no fun."

"I just can't believe that no one has come forward about this baby. Not the mother, not the grandparents, nobody."

"It's sad."

"It is."

We chatted a while until the food arrived. Kirk reached over with his chopsticks and grabbed a piece of my sushi. "Hey!" I protested.

"You want one of mine?" he asked, mouth full.

"Ugh, fish eggs. No, thanks."

He paid the bill when we were finished, and we agreed to meet the next morning at the O'Dell's apartment. I went home to find Grant making spaghetti. The table was set with nice napkins and candles.

"Wow, what's the occasion?" I asked, after a kiss and pouring myself a glass of wine.

"No occasion, just thought it was a good night for a romantic dinner."

The sushi sat in my stomach like a rock. "Smells yummy."

"Hope you're hungry."

I choked down a plate of pasta and a piece of garlic bread and told Grant a bit about the case. All of the details we talked about were already on the news. "So, we don't know who the mother is, or anything. They haven't released the name of the man who was killed yet."

"I'm surprised they identified him so fast, if at all. That's hard to do after an explosion."

"Ugh." My stomach churned. "Yep."

"I thought after 9/11 it was virtually impossible to find enough explosives to make a bomb."

"Not to mention after Timothy McVeigh and Oklahoma City. You can find them though. You can buy small amounts of fertilizer without much trouble."

"Like what?"

"Ammonium Nitrate, for example. Less than forty pounds would blow up a room."

I glared at him. "How do you know all this?"

"I read. That's all."

"Where would you get this stuff? Ammonium…"

"Nitrate. Also known as ANFO, for Ammonium Nitrate and Fuel Oil. You can buy the Ammonium Nitrate at farm supply places. The fuel oil is used up north to heat houses. I imagine if you bought a large amount of it, someone would notice."

"You are kind of scaring me a little."

Grant laughed. "I don't want to blow you up. Yet."

We snuggled on the couch and watched a movie before hitting the sack. I was sound asleep when my phone rang at two in the morning. I knew who it was.

It took me a minute to grab the phone and answer, "Leah, you have got to stop this. I need a good night's sleep."

"LaReesa's here."

I sat up. "What?"

"She literally just walked up and knocked on the door. Bout scared the mess outta me. She's looking for you. And Claire, listen, she doesn't look good. Somebody's worked her over."

"I'll be right there."

Chapter Three

Why don't these kids ever show up in the middle of the day? I asked myself as I raced to the office. I'd seen plenty of kids here in the middle of the night, hunched over in the chair by Leah's desk, looking lost and forlorn and abandoned and scared. But LaReesa was different. I experienced a rush of emotions stronger than usual as I pulled up to the building. Anger, relief, curiosity. I sat in the car for a moment and tried to control myself. I didn't want to bust in there yelling and screaming, as tempting as that was. She'd leave again if I did.

She looked up when I entered. Her left eye was a little swollen, and that cheekbone was bruised like someone had backhanded her, hard. Every time I'd seen her before, her hair had been beautifully styled in an elaborate up-do with lots of curls. Now it was pulled tight back in a ponytail and looked rough and brittle. A bit of dried blood dripped down her white shirt, like she'd had a nosebleed. Her makeup was absent. God, she'd really been through it.

"Hi," she said as I walked in the door.

"Hi."

She stood up and I opened my arms. Her arms wrapped around my waist in a tight hug. We stood like that for a couple of minutes, both of us trying hard not to lose it. She smelled musty, like it had been a while since she'd bathed. Finally, Leah cleared her throat. "She's already been to court with an officer and one of my workers. I was going to place her at a foster home, but she asked for you. I see we don't have an open case on her," Leah said.

"No." I turned to LaReesa. "I need to talk to you about your grandmother."

"She's dead."

I was startled. "You know that? How do you know that?"

"Word gets around." "Your cousins are in foster care. If you want, I can try to get you placed--"

"No! I don't want to go live with those babies."

"But they're your family."

"I don't care. My damn family ain't never done nothin' for me. My stupid-ass mom done got herself locked up, and my aunt the same. Fuck 'em."

"LaReesa."

"I wanna live with you."

Leah made a little choking sound in her throat. I shot her a look and said to LaReesa, "Hey, let me go talk to Ms. Knighton for a minute, okay? Can you wait here for a minute?"

"Where the hell else I gonna go?"

"I'll be right back." Leah and I excused ourselves and walked out to the back lobby. The security guard nodded to us both and went to do his rounds.

I faced Leah and took a deep breath. "I'm going to bring her home with me tonight, and go from there tomorrow."

"You have lost your damn mind. That's against policy and you know it. You're endangering your job. Do you have any idea the risk you're taking? That kid's been on the street, high on only God knows what, and you want to bring her into your home? You're crazy."

"She's really got no one else."

"Well then who's she been with?"

That was a good question. I was silent for a minute, giving Leah a chance to continue with, "And what about Grant? Don't you think you should discuss this with him? You're really putting him at risk."

Damn. Grant. I hadn't even thought about his role in this. I did need to talk with him, but it was three in the morning and I was more worried about tonight.

"Look, Claire, I appreciate your kind heart and your feelings for this poor girl, but I can't sanction this. If Director Pope ever heard that I--"

"Yeah, yeah I know." I could feel anger starting in my gut. "Gotta worry about the goddamn bureaucracy and not the kids." I regretted it the moment I said it.

She gasped. "Really? I'm here every night taking care of whatever comes in the door, and you're gonna—screw you, Claire. Screw you."

"I'm sorry, I'm just frustrated. She's kinda stolen my heart."

"She'll likely steal a lot more than that before this is over. How are you going to get her in school if you don't have custody? And what if she needs medical care? Someone has got to have custody of this kid, even if it's the state of Alabama. And Grant really needs to okay this."

"I know."

"You're in way over your head. Kids are expensive. And DHS can provide services if you need them, you know. You may need us."

"I know. But I'm not a licensed foster parent. For legal reasons

I may not get her without that."

"Look, I think it's going to take me a few days to get all the paperwork done. That will give you time to talk to an attorney. And Mac."

I smiled. "Thanks. I'm sorry about what I said."

"I know. I still think you've gone off the deep end."

"Maybe."

LaReesa was waiting in the chair when we returned. She looked as exhausted as I felt. "Okay, Reese, here's the deal. You're going to come home with me for tonight, maybe for the next few days. Is that okay?"

She smiled. Her teeth were still too large for her face and a little crooked. "That's great!"

"Have you got any stuff with you? Any clothes?"

"No."

"Nothing?"

"I had to leave in kinda a hurry."

We headed to the car. "Listen, you know that boyfriend of mine you heard about when I saw you last?"

"Yeah."

"Well, he and I live together now."

"Is he nice?"

"I think so. He's going to have to approve all this, you know, so I'd be real nice to him. In an appropriate way, of course."

"By the way, I ain't on no drugs, no matter what that bitch back there said."

"You were listening to our conversation?" "Yeah, from behind the guard's desk."

I sighed. "We are going to have to work on you minding your own business."

"This is my business. Y'all were talkin' bout me."

I laughed. "True enough. Listen, it's going to take me a couple days to get things worked out, but you're going to have to go back to school, you know."

"Why?"

"Because you need more than an eighth-grade education and a cute face to get through life." I took the Alford road exit and turned right toward Bluff Park.

"What school will I go to?"

"Goodwin Middle School, most likely." She'd probably have to repeat the eighth grade, but I didn't want to get into that now. Ten minutes later I pulled into my driveway and parked in the carport.

Grant's van was at the curb.

"Can I take a shower?"

"Of course. Just try to be quiet. Grant's asleep."

I found her clean towels and washcloth and waited for the water to turn on. Reese was a big girl, chunky and pear-shaped, and I doubted any of my clothes would fit her. When Grant moved in, he'd collected a bunch of old t-shirts that he no longer needed. They had been in a bag in my laundry room because neither of us had found the time to drop them off at Goodwill. I found a grey Iron Bowl tee from a few years ago with a small hole in the armpit. Grant wore an extra-large tall, so the shirt would come to her knees, at least.

She came out of the hall bathroom in a towel, with another wrapped around her head. I gave her the tee and showed her the guest room before throwing her clothes in the washer. I had a double bed in the guest room, currently stacked with my clean laundry and miscellaneous junk. I moved it all to the office and told her there were clean sheets on the bed.

The walls in the bedroom were a light yellow, and the comforter blue and yellow floral. Reese took it all in as she pulled the shirt over her head. "This nice."

"Thanks."

"For an ol' lady. Can I paint it orange?"

"Orange?"

"That's my favorite color."

"I thought you liked pink."

"I do, jus' not as much as orange."

"Let's worry about the décor later. Get some sleep." I tucked her into bed. "We'll go tomorrow and get you some clothes, okay? I have to go to work tomorrow but we'll go out tomorrow night."

She was drifting off. "K. Claire?"

"Yeah?"

"Thanks for lettin' me stay here."

"Get some rest."

I went out to the living room and called Mac. Left him a message stating I'd be in late. I left it vague on purpose. The sun would be rising in a couple of hours as I slid into bed beside Grant. He groaned and wrapped his warm arms around me. "You 'k?"

"I am. I had a work emergency. By the way, there's a thirteen-year-old girl in the guest room."

"Har erm." He muttered.

I left it at that.

Chapter Four

I woke up to LaReesa screaming.

I jumped out of bed, threw on my robe and rushed to the hall. Reese was in the bathroom, and Grant was in the hall, red-faced and stammering.

"What the hell, man? I was on the toilet!"

"I—I'm so sorry. I just wanted to get my razor. I had no idea you were in there. I didn't see anything, I swear."

I interceded. "Grant, this is LaReesa. Reese, this is Grant."

"Yeah, we've met," Grant said.

"I need coffee," I stated.

I made my way to the kitchen and poured myself a mug. Grant followed me. "So, how long is she going to stay here?"

"Good question. All of the adults in her family are either in prison or dead. I don't really want to put her in foster care right now because I think she'll run. So she's with me for now."

"Does Mac know about this?"

"Not exactly."

"Are you going to tell him?"

"Um..."

"Claire--"

"Grant, this all went down starting at about two in the morning. -I've had" - I checked the clock on the microwave behind me - "two and a half hours of sleep. Some of this was reactionary, I know. And I'll bring Mac into it when the time is right. She's a thirteen-year-old girl and she's really nice when you get to know her."

"Is she going to go to school?"

"Of course, eventually."

"Are you working today?"

"Yeah, I have a meeting at ten."

"So what is she going to do today? Are you going to leave her here alone?"

Leah's comment about her stealing from me flitted through my mind and I didn't answer.

"I tell you what, I'll take her to the shop. Maybe she likes computers. If nothing else, I can let her game while I work."

"You're an angel."

"I wish you'd talked to me before bringing her here."

"Like I said, it was two in the morning and I was out of options." I yawned. "I really need some more sleep."

Grant slid his long arms around me in a soft hug and kissed my forehead. I breathed deep, loving the way he smelled. Reese peeked in the kitchen.

I pulled away and addressed her, "Hey. You want to go back to sleep for a while?"

"What's going on today?"

"I have to go to work at ten for a while. I'm going to drop you off at Grant's shop while I do that. Do you like computers?"

"Yeah."

Grant said, "Great, I could really use some help. Right now, I've got to get to the shop." He kissed me goodbye and was gone with a "See you later."

"I'm hungry," Reese announced. I rummaged through the fridge and freezer and in the end toasted her some frozen waffles and poured her some orange juice. I put her clothes in the dryer, then I went back to bed for an hour while Reese ate and watched TV.

I struggled out of bed at eight thirty and got ready. Reese was dressed and was dozing on the couch. I woke her up and we drove to Grant's shop, High Tech. He was there with two of his employees, Mamik and Regina. We got Reese settled behind a PC and I went to the area of town known as Southside.

Kirk was already there, pacing in the parking lot.

"Calm down, I'm five minutes early."

"I know, it's just excess energy." He kissed my cheek and then ducked away like I was going to slap him. "Sorry. It's my habit to kiss a pretty girl on the cheek."

I laughed. "You're okay."

The police officer was standing at the door, looking bored. We approached him and I introduced myself, showed my ID and asked if I could get some clothes and things for the baby. Kirk stood nearby, trying not to look that interested. Hopefully the guard would assume he was a child welfare worker, like me. The officer radioed somebody who gave the okay, and he opened the door and followed us inside.

The apartment was fairly nondescript. The walls were off-white and held no posters or art. The carpet was a worn beige. One old, brown leather sofa was against the long wall flanked by two wooden end tables. The drawers in the end tables were open and had been searched. A 50-inch TV sat on a stand opposite. Not a lot of clutter, either. One large, plastic tub partially full of toys sat in a corner and I picked that up and handed it to Kirk, who took it without comment. A hallway led to two bedrooms and a bathroom. The first door revealed Jason's bedroom. One king-sized bed, unmade, with navy blue sheets and no bedspread. I glanced at the policeman beside me and closed the door, then opened the other.

This is more like it, I thought. The walls were a light, pretty pink and cutouts of butterflies climbed the wall behind the white crib. Matching butterfly sheets and a soft pink blanket lay in the crib, along with a variety of stuffed animals. I gathered them and added them to the tub that Kirk was carrying. A white rocking chair sat by the window, next to a changing table on top of a dresser. The dresser held lots of cute outfits, dresses and shirts and pants, all of which went into the tub. I found a pack of diapers near the changing table and grabbed that too.

A book lay on the seat of the rocking chair, titled *Guess How Much I Love You?* It kicked me in the feels as I thumbed through it. I turned so Kirk wouldn't see me getting emotional. It went into the tub as well. Kirk was studying everything as we walked through the house and I could tell he was wishing the cop would leave us alone. I turned to the officer. "Did anyone find a birth certificate, that you know of?"

"I don't know," he said, and got on the radio again. The mystery man on the other end answered that they had not, and the policeman agreed to let me search. We went back to Jason's bedroom and I started with the closet. Kirk put the tub of stuff on the bed and helped. The closet just revealed clothes and one small suitcase and that was it. No filing cabinet was visible in the house at all, and I wondered where he would have kept his important papers. I voiced this curiosity to Kirk, who also had no idea.

We searched all the drawers in the apartment, and the closets, but found nothing. Now I was really intrigued. As Kirk and I loaded my trunk with the now-overflowing tub of clothes and toys, I said, "Well, that's weird. I mean, everyone has a box or a filing cabinet or something where they keep important papers, don't they? Your birth certificate, marriage license, that sort of thing?"

"I would think so. What's next?"

"I'm going to put the records department on the case, look for a birth certificate."

"Will you keep me posted?" he whispered.

"I will," I whispered back.

We said goodbye and I took the box of stuff to the Davidson's house, then went back to the office. Kirk had the decency not to follow me. It was close to lunchtime and I hoped I hadn't missed Michele. She was a close friend who helped run our records department. Her office was a glass-enclosed booth, left over from when our building had been the Barwick's Department store. I entered and sat on the chair next to her desk.

"What's up?" she asked as she typed.

"I need to find a birth certificate for a kid."

She handed me the form, and I sat where I was and filled it out with all the information I had. The daycare had told me that Maddie's birthday was April 24th of last year, and I included that on the form. I signed it and handed it back to Michele, who said she'd call me later with what she could find. I asked about her kids. Her son Ian was nearly seventeen, taking the ACT, and looking at colleges. It looked like Auburn was in the lead. I made small talk for a while with Michele, dreading the next task I had to perform.

I took the elevator back to my floor and knocked on Mac's door. He growled a "Come in," and I thought about just turning around and never coming back. He was buried in paperwork, as usual, and stacks of files were piled up on all the chairs. The agency had talked for years about going all-digital, but so far had not made a lot of progress in that area. I often wondered how Mac would react if that ever happened. He gestured to a stack with the unlit cigar he carried with him everywhere. "Jus' move that to the floor."

I did, and sat where he indicated. He signed off on one last form and focused on me. "What's going on?"

"You know that case that Leah called you about last night?"

"Yeah, the thirteen-year-old? What about her?"

"Her name is LaReesa Jones and, well, she's kind of living with me."

Mac never yelled. I could say that for him, he never yelled. I was convinced that fact was going to give him a heart attack one day soon. He studied my face in stern silence and I could practically hear him counting to ten. Then to twenty.

"Why? You know that's against policy."

"I know her. From last year. Remember the Samantha Chambless case?"

"Of course."

"I met her when I was investigating that case. She was hanging out in a parking lot instead of going to school. I got to know her a bit." I stopped there.

"Aren't her cousins in our care?"

"Yes, she has three younger cousins in foster care: DeCora, DeCaria, and DeCameron Jones. Her mother and her aunt are in prison, and her grandmother died in November. There's no other family."

That look again. I stared at the floor and said, "When we have kids come into care, if a family friend wants to take them, we've placed them there before. How is this different?"

"How long do you intend to keep this up? Can she stay with you a week? A year? Four years? Five years? Are you willing to file for custody?"

"I'm kinda taking it day by day."

"What's Grant say about it?"

"We haven't really had the chance to talk in depth yet."

"This may turn out to be a big commitment."

"I know."

More silence. I stared at the scuffed tile floor, totally uncomfortable, and dreaded what he was going to say.

"I will have to let Dr. Pope know about this, and she may not agree to it. You will keep me informed about how she is doing. You will let me know if you need help."

"Yes, sir."

"What's going on with the Madeline O'Dell case?"

"I went to her father's apartment this morning and picked up a few of her things. She's with the Davidsons and doing well. I've got Michele looking for a birth certificate and any other documentation. Shelter care hearing is Friday."

He dismissed me and I could tell he was not happy, but at least he hadn't ordered me to give LaReesa up. I closed his door with a sigh of relief and made my way back to my cubicle. Russell was out. I thought about what to do next. After mulling it over, I decided to go home. I had to get Reese some clothes this evening and if I was honest, I could've used a nap. I packed up some things to work on later and headed to Grant's shop.

Reese was at a PC, playing a game of Solitaire on the monitor and nibbling on the last of a box of French fries. Grant greeted and kissed me when I walked in the door. "How's it going?" I asked.

"She's been fine, just playing away."

"Reese? You ready to go? How about we go shopping?"

"Let me finish this game."

"Five minutes."

I chatted with Grant and Mamik while she played. Regina, his other employee, was monitoring the phones. After five minutes I called to Reese, "Let's go. Don't you want to go shopping?"

That got her off the game. I kissed Grant goodbye and we headed for the shopping center not too far from my house that contained a Target and Kohls.

"So," I said, "one of the things we have to get today is something for you to wear to court."

"Court! What for? I ain't done nothin'!"

"Reese, you're a minor, and someone has to have custody of you even if it's the State of Alabama. You're not in trouble. You just have to go meet the judge and let him put you in the State's custody. No biggie."

"Why can't you get custody of me?"

"Well, that might happen in the future. For now, it will be the State."

"I can still live with you?"

"As far as I know, yes. I told my boss about this today and he didn't say no."

"Good."

"But I have to get the court papers to get you in school."

"But I don't wanna--"

I stopped her there. "You wanna live with me, you have to go to school. No choice. End of chat."

She sulked for the rest of the way to Kohls, but brightened up when we entered. "I can get whatever I want?"

"You can get five outfits. And something for court, remember. And you need bras and undies, too. And pajamas or something to sleep in."

"Does it have to be a dress, for court?"

"No, just something nice, like you'd wear to church."

We spent an hour in the store while Reese looked over what seemed like every bit of clothing in the place. I had to call her down, twice, for picking out shirts that were too tight and too low cut for school, or anyplace else for that matter. She found five outfits she liked, including a skirt and top for court. I sat by the dressing room and waited while she tried it all on.

My phone rang. Work. It was Michele.

"So there's no birth certificate for Madeline O'Dell."

"What?"

"Nothing. No O'Dell's born on April 24."

"That's odd."

"Yep. I've got some calls in to other states, Mississippi, Georgia, Tennessee. We'll see what comes up."

"Okay, thanks."

I hung up. That was a surprise and I wondered who she was and where she was born. My phone rang again. Damn, I thought, what now?

The number was Dad's home number. I answered.

"What's up?"

"Claire? I need to see you as soon as possible. Can you come over?"

He sounded upset, tense. "What's the matter?"

"I'm fine. Just come over."

"I'll be there as soon as I can."

I hustled LaReesa out of the dressing room and hurried to pay for the clothes. "Whas' wrong?" she asked. I completed the transaction as she asked again. And again. When we were in the car, I told her my father had called and needed me right away. I dropped her back at Grant's store, much to his surprise. I explained and he sweetly agreed to watch her while I went to Dad's.

My father's house - the house where I grew up - sat on the ridgetop of Shades Mountain and had a gorgeous view of the area known as Jones Valley. It was about five minutes from where I currently lived. I sped up Tyler Road into Bluff Park and pulled up to his house, noting the extra Cadillac SUV next to his Prius in the driveway. I didn't bother knocking, just walked in the door.

Dad was in the living room with a black man. He was average height with a slight belly, and bald with a short gray beard. He was casually dressed in a yellow golf shirt and jeans. I couldn't help but think I'd seen him before. Dad stood beside him. "Claire, I don't think you've met Dr. Marcus Freedman?"

I laughed as I shook his hand. "I was trying to think why you looked familiar. I'm used to seeing you in a suit, on the news."

"Yeah, it's nice to have a break from the ties."

Dad gestured to the sofa and suggested we all sit down. Marcus and I sat on the couch and Dad sat in his favorite ancient leather recliner opposite us.

Marcus looked a bit uncomfortable, and I wondered again about the purpose of this meeting. "I'm so sorry about Jason O'Dell," I said. "Were you very close to him?" A weird look passed across his face. "A little. Not...I understand you have custody of his daughter?"

"She's in foster care, yes."

"How's she doing?"

"She's fine. I haven't heard from any of Jason's family yet, and it's my understanding the authorities haven't been able to locate them. Do you know how to get in touch with them?"

Another weird look and uncomfortable silence. I turned to

Dad. "What's going on?"

"Marcus," Dad said.

"I know."

Marcus looked at me and I was surprised to see tears in his eyes. "Maddie's my granddaughter."

Chapter Five

Whoa.

I took a deep breath and tried to remember what I knew about Marcus from the media. He was married, his wife was named Betty Ann, and I couldn't remember a mention of any children. "Your granddaughter?"

"My daughter was her mother."

"Was?"

"Was."

"I'm sorry."

The tears were really flowing now, running down his face and dripping on the yellow polo, leaving dark yellow spots. Dad handed him a tissue. "We've worked so hard to keep this out of the media. I just don't know what I'm going to do."

"What happened?"

"On her death certificate, it says cardiac arrest."

"But?"

"But it was secondary to opioids and other drug abuse. She was barely twenty-one. I really thought Jason would help keep her clean. He loved her so much. He was living as Jason O'Dell to hide from-- everyone. And then when she got pregnant, I thought maybe she would get clean for the baby."

He was hitting me with a lot of information. I took a second to absorb it all. "Jason's real name was what?"

"Jason Alsbrook."

"Alsbrook? As in, like, *the* Alsbrooks?"

"Yes."

The Alsbrooks were a very wealthy family, known to just about everyone who lived here. Most of their money had been made in coal mining. They owned at least three mines in Alabama that I knew of, and were regular contributors to charities in the area, including the Children's Hospital and the Museum of Art. If I remembered correctly, there was a wing at the hospital that bore the Alsbrook name. I wondered how this elite Mountain Brook family had reacted when their son hooked up with a black drug addict, daughter of an aspiring professor or not.

"So, has anyone called them about Jason's death?"

"I spoke to James, his father, yesterday and told him what happened. Jason was living as an O'Dell to stay hidden, mostly from the media. He dropped out of UAB when Tameka got pregnant. He was really trying to do the right thing."

Marcus dried his tears and focused on me. "Can I see my granddaughter? Betty Ann and I would love to see her."

"You can have custody of her if you like. Legally, you have first rights."

"I'll have to talk to Betty Ann about that. I mean, a nearly nine-month old is a lot of work."

"The same goes for the Alsbrooks, too, as far as custody goes. I'll need to talk to them." I sincerely hoped this wouldn't turn into a nasty battle.

"I just don't know what I can do to keep this off the airwaves. I've worked so hard in this mayoral race, and I don't want to screw that up."

"But this is your grandchild, your last living relative…"

"I know." The tears were flowing again. He dabbed at his eyes with the tissue. His cell phone chimed from his pocket and he fished it out. "Excuse me," he said, and stepped outside onto the deck.

I looked at Dad. "Did you know all this?"

"Not until this morning. He called me because he knew I had a daughter who was a child welfare worker at DHS. He was hoping you'd have information about Maddie."

"I hope he, or the Alsbrooks, want custody of her. That would make my life a lot easier."

"You look tired."

"I didn't get a lot of sleep last night."

"Do I want to know the details?"

I laughed. "I need to tell you about it. Not today, though. But soon."

"How's Grant?"

"He's fine. Busy. We're both busy."

Marcus returned from the deck. "Sorry. Work. I've got to hire someone to replace Jason pretty quick. He was my campaign manager."

"Are his parents arranging for his funeral?"

"I think so. They are going to call and claim the body. Then it's going to hit the media. Oh, God."

I had a sudden idea. "Dr. Freedman, what if you did an interview and got out ahead of this thing? I have a good friend at the *News* and I could get him here pretty quickly. Might give you some control over the story." And, I thought to myself, Kirk would owe me big time.

"I wouldn't know who to trust. They would have to understand about Tameka…"

"My friend is very good. I think he'll be gentle, not treat this as tabloid fodder."

"That's probably a good idea."

"Let me call him."

I stepped out to the deck where Marcus had been moments ago. Dad had re-stained it last summer to a pretty cedar color and it looked great. I shivered as I perched on one of the mesh outdoor chairs and called Kirk.

"Hey, Beautiful, what's up?"

"My head is reeling and I need you here right now."

"Ooh, this sounds fun."

"Seriously, please drop whatever you are doing and come to my dad's house. This is going to be a hell of an interview."

"Where are you?"

I gave him the address, and he said he'd be there in fifteen minutes. I went inside, where Dad was clearing the kitchen table and filling glasses of water for everyone. Marcus sat at the table and I told him Kirk would be here in just a few minutes.

"Kirk Mahoney?"

"That's right."

"I've talked to him a couple of times. He seems nice."

"He is, and he can keep a secret when asked."

Marcus excused himself and went to bathroom to wash his face. By the time he rejoined us, Dad had wiped the table and a few minutes later the doorbell rang. I answered it.

Kirk was dressed in a business shirt and tie, and gray pants with a heavy black overcoat. I'd never seen him so dressed up. The shirt was light blue and the tie was navy. A digital camera hung around his neck. He looked nice and I told him so. "I know," he said with a wink and I rolled my eyes and stepped outside, closing the door behind me.

"What's this about?" he asked.

"Marcus Freedman is here and you won't believe his story. First, Jason O'Dell's real name is Jason Alsbrook."

"Alsbrook, as in…"

"Yes. And Marcus is Jason's daughter's grandfather."

"What?"

"He'll tell you about it, but I need you to be cool."

"Cool?"

"Sympathetic. Empathetic. Don't turn this into, I don't know…"

"Sensationalism?"

"Yes, that's it."

"Have I ever?"

I thought for a second and realized he never had. "No, I guess not."

"That's why you love me."

"Try again."

"Like me?" He said it with a cute smile.

I chuckled, softly. "Come on in and I'll introduce you."

I led him to the kitchen where Marcus and Dad sat and introduced everyone. Marcus was fidgeting with his keys and looked nervous. Kirk sat down next to him and thanked him for granting him an interview. He asked if he could record it and, after Marcus nodded, turned on the recorder on his cell phone.

"I'm just hoping to get ahead of this and get on with the mayoral race. That bombing…"

"Do you have any idea who might have bombed you?" Kirk asked.

"I mean, I get threats all the time. Really horrible stuff, from really ignorant folks. Most of the time the letters aren't even spelled correctly. But I can't really talk about that on the record. The FBI has asked me not to while they investigate."

"Tell me about Jason O'Dell."

"Jason O'Dell's real name was Jason Alsbrook. I really want to leave his part of the story to his parents, if you don't mind."

"Sure. He worked for you, but did you have a relationship with him outside of work?"

Marcus took a deep breath, and his voice broke as he spoke. "I had a daughter. Her name was Tameka Alexis Freedman. She died seven months ago." Dad handed Marcus another tissue. "She was twenty-one."

Something had happened with Kirk. His face was serious, but kind. I had never seen him like this. He reached over and briefly clasped Marcus's arm. "I'm so sorry."

"I want to tell her story."

"Of course. Go ahead."

"Tameka was a smart kid. She did well in school and she was so popular. Until her senior year of high school. She fell in with some older kids who were into getting high. They'd steal pills from their parents or anywhere they could find them. I mean, at first it was just a little alcohol, then a little weed. We just thought it was a phase she was going through. Like most teens do. Hell, I even drank a bit in high school, you know?"

Kirk nodded, along with me and Dad. "But then the pills started and she just got worse. She started skipping school. Randolph High School said there was a chance she might not graduate because she had missed so many days. We put her into a residential treatment program, one of the places where she had to go and live for, like, six months. She left after four. And she was worse. She made friends in that place who had no intention of staying clean, and they gave her access to even harder drugs. She dropped out of high school two months before she was set to graduate."

Marcus wiped his eyes. "Betty Ann and I stayed in counseling. God, we just needed any help anyone could offer. Finally, when she turned twenty, we decided it was time for tough love. We sat down with the counselor and Tameka and told her she had to go back to treatment or she had to move out." Marcus was crying heavily now, stopping to sob into the tissue. "If I had known she was going to die—if I had known—if I could go back—if only-"

Dad stood up and squeezed his shoulder. Kirk reached over and held his arm again. I felt a lump in my throat and was trying not to lose it.

"I'm so sorry." I said. "Did you know she had a daughter?"

"She got pregnant a while after she moved out. Jason called us to tell us because Tameka refused to speak to us. Jason was a stand-up guy. He wasn't an addict and he wanted her to get help. He really loved her."

"How did they meet? Do you know?" Kirk asked.

"I think Jason had a roommate who was into drugs. He said they met at his old house one night when his roommate had a party. Jason was really frustrated with him and moved out shortly after. Jason was a good kid, interested in the business end of politics. He was hoping for a career in that field. He did a good job of managing my campaign every day."

"What do you want people to know about Tameka?"

"Like I said, she was a smart kid. Funny. I miss her so much. The counselor said she had, an - what did she call it - an addictive personality. She gave us a book. It said some people are more likely to be addicted and there really wasn't much we could have done to stop it. She was going to die or continue to make our lives total chaos. I wish she'd had the will to stop."

"Was your granddaughter born addicted?"

"I don't know. We weren't there when she was born. Tameka

refused to let us be there, but I'm sure she did some drugs when she was pregnant."

I added, "Maddie wasn't born with drugs in her system or we would have been called. We have no prior record on her." I looked at Kirk. "Off the record." He rolled his eyes at me.

"I guess that's some good news," Marcus said.

I had considered the drug question about Maddie before, and needed to schedule a medical check-up for her as soon as the shelter care hearing was completed. If she had been gestated with drugs in her system, we'd see signs pretty quickly. Things like delays in movement and cognitive function. In elementary school, there was a good chance Maddie would show signs of learning disabilities and/or impulse control problems if she'd been born dependent. Hopefully she had avoided all that, but we'd have to wait and see. I mentioned this. If Marcus wanted custody, he had a right to know.

"Do you want custody of Maddie?" Kirk asked, as though he was reading my mind.

"I'm going to have to talk to Betty Ann, since she is the one who will be doing most of the work, but yeah, I think I do. She's the last part of our daughter."

"Was Tameka an only child?"

"She was. Betty had her late in life. She was thirty-four when Tam was born. We had tried for years and she was a very welcome surprise. What do I need to do to get custody?"

"You'll need a lawyer," I answered.

Marcus chuckled. "I have about thirty."

"One who has experience in Family Law. Any of your lawyers should be able to recommend somebody."

"Then what?"

"Tomorrow we're going to have what's called a Shelter Care hearing at Family Court. Judge Myer will hear the case and decide who gets temporary custody, the family or the State. He may require a background check."

"I'll pass that. My background's already been investigated nonstop by the media and my opponent. I've got nothing left to hide."

"Then I'll see you at Family Court. Nine a.m. tomorrow."

I turned to Kirk. "Do you have anything else?"

"Has anything been done to honor Tameka's memory? Sometimes my readers want to give when they hear a story like this."

"I'm in the beginning of setting up a foundation to help parents who have kids with drug issues. I don't really know what we are going to do yet. I'm hoping education and support groups. People can stay tuned and I'll let them know when we are ready for donations."

Kirk snapped a few pictures of Marcus, then they shook hands and exchanged cards. I walked Kirk out to his silver Infiniti. "Wow," he said. "Thanks so much for this. I've got to get back to the office and get this written. I'm also going to track down the Alsbrooks. Do you want to go with me to talk to them?"

"Yeah, of course. But don't you think I should call them? I think they'd react better to a DHS worker than the media, don't you?"

"Good point. You'll call them today?"

"I'll try."

"You look tired." He lifted my chin gently with his forefinger and his sky-blue eyes met mine. Something in my chest quivered gently. "You okay?"

"I was working really late last night. I'm a little sleepy."

"Take care of yourself." He bent and kissed my cheek, and lingered there a bit. I didn't pull away.

"I will. I'll call you later."

He took off in his flashy car and I went back inside. Marcus and Dad were saying goodbye but before Marcus left, I got him to give me James Alsbrook's cell phone number. Dad and I sat in the living room after he left and chatted.

"Kirk's a handsome man," he said. "Is he married?"

"No."

"And you two are…"

"Just friends, Dad. I've got to go make some phone calls and get some sleep."

"Be careful, Claire."

I was being careful. Or so I thought.

Chapter Six

I went home, ate a sandwich, and slept like the dead for fourteen hours, coming to consciousness only for a moment when Grant and Reese came home later that evening. I woke at seven on Friday morning and quickly finished the court report for Madeline Freedman's case. I was asking for Madeline to be placed with her maternal grandparents with a three-month review. I was also asking the judge the leave the case open with DHS so that we could complete our assessments and get her any services she might need. I also needed time to talk to the Alsbrooks.

Kirk's story was in the paper, too. It was the lead story on the front page, the headline a quote from Marcus. "I've Got Nothing Left to Hide" it proclaimed, and the story was a tender account of Tameka's life. Kirk had called Betty Ann and gotten a couple of quotes from her about her daughter along with a photo. She talked about how they were looking forward to spending time with their new granddaughter. *Better luck this time*, I thought. DHS and my name weren't mentioned.

I was at Family Court by nine a.m., and met with the DHS attorney, along with Marcus and Betty Ann and their attorney in one of the little glass-fronted conference rooms. I explained that this was just a shelter care hearing to determine where Maddie was going to live for the time being, and shouldn't take too long.

The Davidsons arrived with Maddie as we were finishing up. Maddie was dressed in one of the dresses I'd gotten from her Dad's apartment, a pink one with little gray polka dots and a matching hair ribbon. She looked too adorable for words. Betty Ann took her immediately and settled her on her lap, then cooed and talked to her. Maddie cooed back and smiled. I could see the bonding happening.

I went to the magistrate's office and scheduled a shelter care hearing for LaReesa Jones for Monday morning, then returned to the courtroom. Judge Myer heard cases with private attorneys first, so we were at the front of the line. I stood with Marcus and Betty Ann and their attorney and waited while he read the report. He started with me.

"Miss Conover?"

"Yes, sir?"

"Have you contacted the paternal grandparents yet?"

"No, sir, I just found out their identities last evening, and I haven't had a chance to call them yet."

"You'll do that today?"

"Yes, sir, immediately after I leave here."

The DHS attorney had nothing to add. Next Judge Myer questioned Marcus's attorney to make sure everyone understood what was happening. Writing on the order, he said, "The baby Madeline will live with her maternal grandparents, the Freedmans, and will be in the State's custody, under supervision of DHS. Review in three months."

"Thank you, sir."

I scheduled an appointment for Monday afternoon with Marcus and his wife to visit them and the baby. Other members of the press had read Kirk's article, too, and were stationed outside as Marcus and Betty Ann left. I ducked around them as they answered questions and went back to the office. I called James Alsbrook's cell number from the office, thinking I'd have better luck if his caller ID showed the State of Alabama. I was right, and he picked up on the third ring.

"Hello?"

"Mr. James Alsbrook?"

"Yes?"

"My name is Claire Conover and I'm with the child welfare division of DHS. Let me start by saying I'm sorry about your son."

"Thank you. What can I do for you?"

"Were you aware your son had a daughter? DHS has custody of her, currently."

"Yes."

Okay. Not a lot of interest here. "Would you be interested in visiting with her? Or seeking custody of her?"

"No. My son had a child with a drug addict, the daughter of that nigger who's running for mayor."

Wow. Racism was alive in Alabama; I knew that. But it was rare for me to hear it so directly. I struggled for something to say. "But Mr. Alsbrook, now that your son is gone, I'd really like to talk with you about your granddaughter. You're her family and--"

"No. Please don't contact me again." He hung up.

I sighed, feeling sorry for this poor little baby who had virtually no chance of getting to know her father's side of the family. I found my cell phone and called Kirk.

"Hey, I talked to James Alsbrook. He's a treat. He wants nothing to do with Maddie."

"Really? He was totally open to meeting with me."

"You called him?"

"Yep. We are meeting today at three at his house."

"How'd you get his number?"

"I'm an investigative reporter and he's a prominent citizen. Easy peasy. Do you want to come with me this afternoon?"

"Duh."

"Such a stellar vocabulary."

"Please?"

"That's better. Shall I pick you up?"

"I'll meet you in the lot at the back of the building."

"Very subtle."

"Listen, I can't--"

"I know, you can't be seen with me. I've heard this about a million times."

"Sorry. I like my job and I don't want to lose it."

"See you at three."

I did paperwork and scheduled home visits until lunchtime. After lunch I ventured up to Michele's office and filled her in about Maddie. She relaunched the search for Maddie's birth certificate while I waited. She searched under the last name Freedman and got a hit. Madeline Alexis Freedman was born on April 24 of last year. Her parents were both listed: Tameka Alexis Freedman and Jason Alan Alsbrook, ages twenty-one and twenty-two. Michele printed me a copy and I took it to my office to be filed.

At two-thirty, I made my way to the back parking lot and casually got into Kirk's car when he pulled in. He wore another light blue dress shirt that exactly matched his eyes, and dark gray pants. He asked me how my night was as he took off, at top speed, for Mountain Brook.

"It was fine. I got some sleep. I have a thirteen-year-old girl living with me at the moment so life is busy."

"Why?"

"She has nowhere else to go."

"You have a heart of gold. How's Minivan Man feel about that?" He used his nickname for Grant.

"We haven't really had a chance to discuss it much yet."

"And living together is going well?"

"I guess. We see each other a bit more, so that's good, I guess."

"You guess?"

"I mean, it's hard to adjust to living with someone."

"I don't know, I've never done it."

"Never?"

"Not so far. Haven't met the right one."

Mountain Brook was a posh suburb of Birmingham, a maze of

roads lined with expansive houses and lawns. Some were nearly a hundred years old and very elegant. It was easy to get lost here, and within moments I had no idea where I was. "Do you know where you are going?" I asked Kirk.

"No, I just thought I'd drive around until I found it. Yes, I know where I'm going."

We passed a golf course, and within minutes pulled up to a drive with a gate. A gate, for God's sake. There was a small building next to it with a man stationed inside. Kirk pulled up and gave the guard his name, who then checked a clipboard and hit a button to open the imposing wrought-iron fence.

We went up a drive that seemed about a hundred yards long. Trees, bare in the winter sun, arched overhead. I bet in the spring it was gorgeous. "This isn't a house, it's an estate."

"Yeah, that's what forty-two million dollars gets you."

"Wow."

"That's James's latest estimated net worth."

"And Jason walked away from all of it? He must have really loved Tameka."

"Must've."

I briefly considered what it must be like to be that rich. To pay off your house. To buy a new car when you needed one without worrying about the payments. It was depressing.

We rounded a curve and the house came into view. It was huge of course, all brick and painted a weathered white with the drive curving up the hill in front. Thick woods of bare trees formed a backdrop to the estate. Nearby sat a three-car garage. A beautifully arched wooden double door opened, and a black man in a suit exited and opened my car door for me. He explained that he worked for Mr. Alsbrook and would show us inside. We were escorted to a study with dark green wallpaper and a huge stone fireplace that with warm flames crackling inside. In the corner was an intricate, antique wooden gun cabinet, stocked with rifles. Above the fireplace was a ten-point deer head, its vacant eyes staring forward. Kirk and I stood in front of the fireplace, taking this all in, when Mr. Alsbrook entered.

I guessed he was in his late fifties, lean and muscular, and was dressed in a dark gray suit with a white dress shirt. No tie. His hair shone silver, like his cufflinks, and was neatly combed. He in no way resembled a man overcome with grief.

He shook Kirk's hand and ignored me. Kirk noticed and introduced me as his friend. I reminded Mr. Alsbrook that I was from DHS and had called him earlier.

"Oh, yes, of course. About the baby."

"I'd love to meet your wife," I said. He shot me a look. You would have thought I'd asked him for his bank account number. He rang a bell and the same nameless black man arrived and was told to get Mrs. Alsbrook. This whole situation was giving me the creeps and I wanted to leave.

Kirk produced his cell phone and a notebook and asked for an interview with both of them. Mr. Alsbrook agreed but didn't look happy about it. He motioned toward the two leather sofas. Then the door opened and Mrs. Alsbrook walked in.

She was a frail-looking, tiny thing, dressed in a baggy tan dress that didn't do much for her color. Her medium-brown hair was in a bun. She had a touch of make-up on, which didn't do much to enhance her appearance. Her attention was on her husband, who pointed to the part of the couch where he wanted her to sit. She sat, and didn't say a word.

Kirk began by expressing his sympathy about their son. Mr. Alsbrook shrugged and Mrs. Alsbrook, her first name still a secret, teared up.

"Can you tell me about Jason?" Kirk asked.

Mrs. Alsbrook stared at her husband, who turned and nodded to her. "We loved our son very much," she practically whispered. "It's been very difficult." She had a soft voice and I wondered if Kirk's cell phone was able to record any of it.

Kirk continued, "Your son was Marcus Freedman's campaign manager? I understand he was interested in a career in politics?"

James Alsbrook shrugged again. "He was enrolled in UAB for a time, getting a dual degree in Political Science and Business. We never discussed his long-term goals."

Mrs. Alsbrook spoke up. "Yes, he loved what he did for a living. I think he would have enjoyed working in politics."

James shot her a look of such pure anger that made me tense. Kirk noticed it, too. The mood in the room had gone ice cold.

"Do you have any other children?" Kirk asked.

"No," Mrs. Alsbrook whispered. "We weren't able."

James answered. "No, Jason was our only son. I had hoped he would want to take over the family business, but he showed no interest. Especially after he met…what was her name? Tameka Freedman?"

"They had a daughter together."

"Yes, I know."

Mrs. Alsbrook had brightened up a bit. I tried to make a connection and said, "Her name is Madeline. She's eight months old and adorable. The Freedmans are seeking custody of her. If you are interested, we can discuss--"

James cut me off. "No. She is where she needs to be."

"Would you like to visit her?"

Mrs. Alsbrook actually smiled when I said that, all the way up to her eyes, but Jackass James shut her down quickly. "No, we are not interested in Jason's mistake. He threw away his relationship with us when he took up with her. I won't have it." And the smile was gone.

"Tell me some more about your son?" Kirk asked.

"He was a good boy, most of his life, until he fell into the wrong crowd in college. He had friends who dabbled in drugs, and that's how he met Tameka. We tried to encourage him to stay away from her, to try to find someone more appropriate, but he wouldn't listen. Then, thankfully, she died."

Thankfully? It was all I could do not to go off on him. I took a deep breath as Kirk very subtly reached over and touched the small of my back. Mr. Alsbrook turned to me. "Conover? Are you Christopher's daughter, by any chance?"

"I am."

"I knew your grandfather, Charles, as well. He was a fine man."

He wasn't, but I didn't say that out loud. I just smiled politely. Mrs. Alsbrook had retreated back into herself and looked far away.

Kirk asked if the Alsbrooks were doing anything in remembrance of their son, and James said the Alsbrook Foundation would happily accept donations, prompting Kirk to ask, "What does the Foundation do, exactly?"

"We give to local charities, mostly. The Children's Hospital and others."

"And anything for the Mourned Miners?"

James looked startled. "Yes, of course. A bit."

"How much have you given them?"

Things were even more tense now, the mood of the room was back to cold, with an edge. Mrs. Alsbrook looked a bit frightened, and I wondered what the hell the Mourned Miners were. I held my tongue.

"I would have to check with our accountants, but I'm sure--"

"Ten thousand dollars. I checked."

"Well, that's–""Actually a lot less than the fines you've paid to the federal government."

James stood. "This interview is over."

"That's only slightly more than the cost of one funeral."

"Goodbye, Mr. Mahoney." James walked to the door and opened it, glaring at Kirk. I subtly reached in my purse and palmed one of my business cards. I walked over to Mrs. Alsbrook, shook her hand, and told her how nice it was to meet her. She slid the card deftly into her pocket. I prayed she'd call me.

Mr. Alsbrook stood like a ramrod, holding the door. I didn't bother to offer my hand, instead slipped out quietly behind Kirk. The same black man showed us to the door, then actually walked us to the car without a word. He wore a brown suit over his fit body and looked to be in his early forties. I noticed his kind eyes, and I turned to him before I entered the car. "What's your name?"

"Ronald, ma'am. Ronald Cushman. I'm the head of security here at the house."

"How do you like working here?"

"Fine, ma'am. Mr. Alsbrook very generous to me."

"Ronald!" James shouted from the doorway.

"Goodbye, Ma'am."

I slid into the car next to Kirk. He sped away. The gate opened as we approached the guardhouse. I glanced at Kirk. He was pissed. Really pissed. "Whew," I said. "That was--"

"What he deserved. Fuckin' asshole."

"What the hell is the Mourned Miners?"

"A charity formed by his victims."

"Victims?"

"That lovely man, James Alsbrook, holds some records here in Alabama. See, he's had the most mining accidents of any firm, and has been fined the most by the federal government."

"Why doesn't the government shut him down?"

"Good question. But that's not the way it works. The Mine Safety and Health Administration inspects coal mines four times a year. They can recommend things to be fixed or order the mine cleared if things are bad enough. Ol' James there pays the fines but never fixes anything. He's lost thirty-three people over the last twenty years. Mostly through explosions. Nothing was set up to take care of the miners' families in case of a death, so the Mourned Miners was founded after the Warm Creek accident five years ago to help with things like funeral and partial living expenses until the families could get back on their feet. And James has given exactly ten thousand dollars. Out of forty-two fucking million. Those guys died making him rich and that's all he can do."

"That's awful."

"Yep. Hey, what's the deal with your grandfather? Charles? Right? You looked like you were going to throw up when Alsbrook mentioned his name."

"I nearly did."

"Why?"

"Charles was my father's father. He was a member of the White Citizen's Council back in the nineteen-fifties and sixties. Hard core racist. Believed blacks were a sub-species, practically, and that Bull Connor hung the moon. My father rejected all that and got away from it."

"Maybe that's what Jason was trying to do."

"I hope so. By the way, I slipped a card to Mrs. Alsbrook. I hope she calls me."

"You little devil."

"I have some suspicions about her. I think she's being abused."

"Wouldn't surprise me. What makes you think that?"

I shrugged. "I dunno. I've met a lot of abused women. Physically and mentally. There's a look. Not just on their faces but… just the way they are. She was moving stiffly, like she was in pain. And she was wearing a baggy dress. If you have bruises, tight clothes hurt. That kind of thing."

"Wow, I totally missed that."

"You were focused on James, and besides, I'm trained in this sort of thing."

Kirk dropped me off at the office and said goodbye with a kiss to my cheek. I had to admit, I was sort of enjoying spending this much time with him. I picked up my car and knew where my next stop was.

Chapter Seven

I pulled up at my father's house a little before five. He greeted me with a hug and asked if I wanted to stay for dinner. I explained that I couldn't and asked if I could talk to him about a couple of things. We went to the living room.

"What's up?"

"First of all, have you heard from Marcus?"

"He called earlier and said to thank you again for everything. They love having little Maddie."

"I'm glad. I met her other grandparents today, the Alsbrooks. James and his wife."

"Oh. No wonder you look bothered."

"He's a piece of work."

"He's a piece of shit."

I laughed. "Yeah, that too. He mentioned Granddad."

"Yeah, your granddad was good friends with James's father. Same belief system. They kept trying to get us to be friends, but I said no thanks. He's several years younger than I am."

"Good call. Everything about him makes me shiver."

"I know what you mean. He's been like that since high school."

"Like what?"

"A racist bully. He used to torture the black kids. The girls, too. He's really nasty."

"You know it was his son that was killed in the bombing this week?"

"I heard the guy's name, didn't realize it was James's son. Sorry to hear that."

"James and his wife—God, I don't even know her name."

"Patricia."

"They want nothing to do with little Maddie because of the color of her skin. It's really sad. Have you met Patricia?"

"Once, a long time ago. She was a mousy, terrified looking little thing."

"Still is. So, there's something else I need to let you know."

"That sounds frightening."

I laughed. "It's not. I'm fostering a thirteen-year-old girl."

Dad's eyebrows shot up in surprise. "I had no idea you were interested in being a foster parent."

"I wasn't. I mean, not really. I met LaReesa Jones on a case last year. She's really something. Bright and funny."

"And black?"

I was startled. "Yeah. Does that matter? Why does that matter?"

"It doesn't, not to me. But you may get some ugliness from a lot of people. Racism is a deep-seated and real thing here."

"Yeah, I've noticed."

"What does Grant say about this? About fostering?"

"We haven't really talked much about it yet. We've both been busy. I think he's okay with it. You just have to get to know Reese, and she can be really nice. Her grandmother died last fall, and her three cousins are in foster care. Her mother and her aunt are both in prison, so she really has nowhere to go."

"Well, I can't wait to meet her. And you're really sweet to take her in. That's a big commitment."

"That's what Mac said. Do you want to come over for dinner this weekend and meet her? Saturday?"

"I don't have any plans, so that would work."

He updated me on the latest news from Chris, my brother, who was a nurse in Florida before I headed to my house. Grant and LaReesa were both there, pouring over a menu for Chinese food. "What's Lo Mein?" Reese asked.

"Noodles." Grant answered. "LaReesa's never had Chinese food," he said after greeting me with a kiss on the cheek, "So I thought we'd try that for dinner."

"Sounds good. I saw Dad today, and he's coming over for dinner tomorrow. I'll throw something together that can be vegetarian or not."

Grant got LaReesa settled in front of a movie and asked if I would ride with him to pick up the food. I agreed and climbed into the front seat of his van. He headed toward the New China Restaurant that was just down the street.

"We kind of need to talk," he said.

"About Reese? I know this has happened quickly and I'm really sorry I haven't kept you much in the loop. Are you mad?"

"No, no, not about that. Two hundred dollars was missing from my cash box at the store yesterday."

"And you think Reese took it?"

"Who else?"

"I don't know, anyone who was in the store? Did you call the police?"

"No, I wanted to talk to you first."

"Did you ask Reese about it?"

"No, I—"

"Why not? You seem to think she stole it."

"I didn't want to start anything without talking to you first."

"You're afraid of her."

"A little. I saw a bit of her temper a couple of days ago. Claire, she's a handful. And likely a thief."

"Wait a minute, there's no evidence she took the money."

"Who else would have? And how long do you think she's going to live here? Until she graduates high school? If she graduates high school," he scoffed.

"You're making a lot of assumptions about everything." I could feel my own temper rising as my voice got a bit louder.

"And you don't even seem to be worried about the theft," Grant countered.

"I'll talk to Reese."

"Good luck. You're going to need it. Seriously, how long are you going to keep this up?"

"Grant, she literally has nowhere else to go."

"Sure she does. Foster care, like everyone else in her situation."

"Grant…" There were a whole cluster of behaviors that came with kids in The System. And reasons for them. It was going to take days to explain all of them and make him understand, if he was willing to understand. I sat in silence as he parked the van and went inside to pick up the food. He brought the bag out and placed it in the back seat.

Calmly I said, "I know I threw this at you suddenly, and I'm really sorry. I should have talked with you about it first. I suspect, if LaReesa took the money, that she may be planning for the future."

"I don't understand."

"I mean, put yourself in her position. Living on the street with God-knows-who and not enough to eat and not knowing where you are going to sleep that night. Some kids steal and put it aside in case they are ever in that situation again."

"Or they steal to buy drugs."

"True, but I don't think that's LaReesa."

"We'll see."

I sighed. This was going to take some time. "I'll talk to her."

"Thanks."

"Her shelter care hearing is Monday at nine. Do you want to come to court with us?"

"Let me check my schedule, but I think I can. No big projects start this week."

We parked at the house and brought the food inside. Reese was watching TV. She seemed to enjoy her first Chinese food. After dinner,

Grant announced he was going to bed and Reese turned the TV to a movie. I took the remote and paused it.

"What the hell?" she asked.

"Try that again." I said.

"Sorry. Why'd you pause it?"

"I want to ask you about something." I took a deep breath and faced her. "I want you to understand I'm not accusing you of anything."

"Uh, oh."

"Seriously, this is just a question. Grant says two hundred dollars was missing out of his cash box yesterday."

Her voice rose dramatically. "Oh, I get it. The little nigga must've taken it. They all steal, you know."

"LaReesa--"

"I didn't take it!"

"Keep it down, please."

"Why? You think I'm a thief!"

"I don't. Really. Even if you did steal it, which I'm sure you didn't, I think I'd understand. It doesn't make it right though."

"I didn't take it!"

"Well, then we are okay."

"Is Grant mad? Why didn't he fuckin' say anything?"

"Look, Grant has never worked with, or even talked to, anyone with your background. Give him some time and he'll see how you really are--"

"Why does everybody keep saying shit like that? Like, about my *background* and all."

"Because most of the teen girls I take into custody have stolen, and used drugs, and prostituted themselves." I watched her reaction carefully to the last part of my statement. She bit her lip and looked at the floor. Then she said, "So you are just going to lump me in with all them, like a statistic."

"I'm sorry. I shouldn't do that. Did you ever—have to--?"

"Hook?"

"Yeah."

She shrugged. "Kinda."

"What does kinda mean?"

"I knew this guy. He older. I knew him from before. He said I could come and stay with him. Then he said if I wanted to stay, I had to, well, you know. With him and his friends."

"So you did."

"I had no place else to go."

"I know." I drew her to me in a hug. "I'm so sorry you had to go through that."

"Is Grant mad I'm here? Does he want me to go?"

"No, no. He'll be fine. Just give him some time."

Tears were running down her face now. "Thanks for letting me stay here."

"You're welcome." I handed her the remote. "I'm going to bed."

"Can I stay up and watch movies?"

"I don't care, since it's the weekend. You can't when school starts."

She scowled at me.

I crawled into bed quietly next to Grant, who rolled over and wrapped his arms around me. "Everything okay?"

"I talked to Reese."

"I know. I heard."

"She says she didn't take it."

"I know. Do you believe her?"

"I do. I think she knows she's got a good thing here and doesn't want to blow it."

"Okay. Claire?"

"Yeah?"

"I love you."

I snuggled closer to him and muttered into his chest, "I love you, too."

"I guess we'll go from there."

Chapter Eight

Saturday morning the cold spell had broken and it was a practically balmy fifty degrees. LaReesa had fallen asleep on the sofa, the TV remote control on the floor next to the couch. I turned the TV off and visited the Piggly Wiggly, commonly known as the Pig, in my neighborhood. I returned home with all the fixings for tacos. Reese woke up while I was unloading and helped me put the stuff away.

"All this for dinner?"

"My father is coming over for dinner."

"Is he cool?"

"Very."

"Can I have a cell phone?"

"Maybe."

"An iPhone? A new one?"

"Maybe, Reese. Let me see what it's going to cost."

"I mean, I could use it if I'm ever in trouble. It wouldn't be for just texting and stuff."

"I will think about it. Let's get your court hearing over with and get you enrolled in school. I don't have a problem with allowing you to have a phone if you go to school and make an effort with your grades."

The scowl again. "So many rules."

"That's life, kiddo."

"I'm gonna have to redo the goddamn eighth grade, ain't I?"

"Well, you missed literally half of it, so yeah. But you know what? You're a bright girl and I'm sure you can catch up if you apply yourself."

"You think so?"

"I know so."

Dad arrived at five. I handed him a beer and introduced him to LaReesa. She studied him closely. He had light blond hair like mine, mostly faded to grey, and the same blue eyes. His blond hair was longer than mine, and worn in a ponytail. He also had a crescent-shaped scar that went from the corner of his left eye down his cheek. LaReesa noticed it immediately, like most people.

"Whoa, shit! You get in a knife fight?"

Dad chuckled. "Something like that. I got beaten up by the cops in 1961."

"You? A white dude? What the hell'd you do?"

"I was with a group of people trying to get equal rights for black people."

"Why? That ain't yo problem."

"Sure it is. The way African-Americans were treated in this country was horrendous. Still is, really. It has to change."

Reese studied the scar again. "Was it worth it?"

"I think so."

I thought of a question. "Dad, I never asked you what Granddad said after you got punched."

"Oh, he was furious. Didn't understand why a young man would want to go out and get hurt trying to get rights for blacks. Of course, he didn't call them blacks. He said it was ridiculous."

I could see Reese getting agitated. I heard her mutter, "Bastard," under her breath. She noticed I heard her and muttered, "Sorry."

"No, you are not wrong. My grandfather had some evil, evil beliefs. Things are still bad, and need to get better."

I made some taco meat and laid everything out on the kitchen counter, buffet style. Dad was a vegetarian today and made himself a veggie taco. LaReesa loaded her plate with three tacos and a side of refried beans. She looked at Dad and asked, "You ain't eatin' no meat? It's good."

"No, I'm a vegetarian," he replied.

I scoffed.

"Well, most of the time," he added.

"Why?"

"I don't want anything to die to feed me. And I can live on vegetables. It's healthier anyway."

"But meat is yummy."

"That's the problem."

We gathered around the dining room table and dug in. Reese bombarded Dad with a million questions about what I was like as a child and at her age, and by the end of the meal they had formed a funny friendship that mostly revolved around picking on me. They liked each other; I could see. Dad asked her at one point, "So where do you come from?"

"I grew up over in Midfield. My mamma, she were a ho and she got locked up. I went and lived with my Granny and my cousins. My Grandma had my little cousins because my aunt, she on drugs. Well, she was. She in prison now, too."

"What about your dad?"

Reese shrugged. "I dunno who he is. Reckon my mamma didn't know neither. I ain't never met him."

"What grade are you in?" Dad asked.

"I was in eight, but I didn' go to school this year. Claire say I gotta go after we go to court on Monday. I'll probably have to repeat eight." She looked a little dejected at this statement.

"You know, you seem really, really smart. I bet you'll do well." LaReesa brightened up at that.

I walked Dad out to his hybrid car after dinner. "You're right," he said, "She's charming."

"I think so."

"And Grant's okay with this?"

"He hasn't said he's not. We still have to find time and privacy to discuss everything."

"Good luck."

LaReesa and Grant did the dishes and I had an early night. The next day I schlepped LaReesa up to Target to shop for new bedding. She picked out a comforter that was light orange and gray in a nice chevron pattern. "An' we can paint the walls orange?" she asked.

"You know, I'd rather not. I may want to sell that house someday and orange isn't everybody's favorite color. What's another choice?"

"How about this gray?" she asked, pointing to the comforter.

"I think that would be perfect."

"Can we go look at paint?"

"Yep."

We walked back to the hardware department and I studied the paint display, comparing the gray shades to the comforter in my cart. "How about this one?" Paint strip in my hand, I turned to face LaReesa.

She was gone.

"LaReesa?" I called. Damn it.

I wheeled the cart toward the other side of the store, looking down all the aisles. I was starting to get a little nervous. Why would she run, I wondered? Why now? Because court was tomorrow? What was she afraid of?

"LaReesa? LaReesa? Reese?" I was trying not to get too loud in the store. I walked through the bath towels and forward into the electronics department, calling her name as loud as I dared, until I heard, "Over here."

I sighed with relief as I approached her. She was studying a display of cell phones.

"I like this one," she said, pointing to an iPhone. The price tag said four hundred and fifty-six dollars. I nearly choked.

"No. No. No."

"Why not?"

"That is way, way, way out of my budget."

"Really?"

"Really. Let's go home and look online. And don't forget, Grant is an expert in all of this stuff. He can really help you pick out something nice. And listen, if you want leave my side to go look around, let me know, okay?"

We went back to the paint section and Reese agreed with my selection of a light gray paint. We also picked out a pretty printed bookbag for her, and some notebooks, under protest. We bought it all and headed home.

Grant was an angel and had moved all the furniture in Reese's room to the center and covered it with tarps while we were gone. He had changed into old clothes, and proved because of his height of six-four, he could paint without tape. He started near the ceiling while I taped the baseboards.

"What do I do?" Reese asked.

"As soon as I get this done, you'll grab a roller."

Five hours later, the sun was down and Reese had a light gray bedroom, with only a tiny bit of gray on the tan carpet. Reese and I made the bed with her new bed set, and I had to admit, it looked really good. We got cleaned up and I helped Grant move the rest of the furniture back. "Thanks for your help today," I said to him.

"No problem. She asked me about a cell phone. What do you think?"

"I told her it was okay if I could afford it. She likes an iPhone that's nearly five hundred bucks and I put the kibosh on that."

He laughed, "She asked me to help her pick out something. I told her we'd talk tonight. I'm not going to recommend an iPhone though."

"Why not?"

"That's a Mac product, an Apple. I don't work with Mac products, usually. It'll be easier to do stuff with it on your PC if you get her an Android. They are cheaper, too. Especially if we buy a refurbished one."

"You didn't tell me any of this when I got an iPhone."

"Yeah, but you use yours for like, a phone."

I laughed. "Guilty. I guess my age is showing."

He reached out and grabbed me in a hug and seductively nibbled my neck. "You still got it, old lady."

My hands reached up and stroked the front of his chest. He

kissed me long and deep and I tried not to think about what would have happened if LaReesa wasn't home. I groaned and said, "I have to go heat up dinner."

"I'm on cell phone duty. What's our budget?"

"I have to find out how much it's going to be to add her to my plan."

"If you limit the data, it shouldn't be bad."

"Would two hundred be enough, for the phone?" I asked.

"Easy."

"Let's go with that, then."

Grant and Reese spent the rest of the evening huddled around his laptop, looking and phones and deals and discussing things I barely understood. After dinner I left them to go write LaReesa's court report for the morning. I didn't have an attorney yet, but I would need one in the future. Soon. It felt weird to be working with my name at the top of the form.

The next morning, I woke early. I got showered and dressed in a somber black suit and was packing my briefcase when Grant walked out in a charcoal gray suit and burgundy tie. He looked amazing and I told him so. He fidgeted with his tie and ran his finger around his neck. "I started my own business so I wouldn't have to wear these freakin' things."

"Too bad, you look good in them."

LaReesa appeared in the skirt and top we'd gotten for court. Her hair looked healthier and was neatly combed. "I look okay?"

I assured her that she did, and on the way to court we discussed what was going to happen. "I would advise that you don't speak unless Judge Myer speaks to you first," I said. "Be humble and grateful. If he says something you don't like, swallow it and don't say a word."

"What's he gon' say that I don't like?"

"He's probably going to order you to stay in school if you want to live with me."

"Well, duh, you already tol' me that. I'm too young to drop out anyways."

"Let's not think about dropping out."

We arrived at Family Court a few minutes early. The lobby was already crowded with families waiting to see the Judge. I left Grant and Reese there and stepped into the courtroom.

There was a surprise waiting for me there.

Chapter Nine

Standing close to the bench were two men in suits, shaking hands and talking like old friends who hadn't seen each other in years: My boss, Mac McAlister, and my father. Dad had been a practicing psychologist in Birmingham for years, but was mostly retired now. He and Mac had known each other for a long time, a fact I often forgot. My jaw dropped in shock as I approached them. Dad wrapped his arm around me in an informal hug. "What are you doing here?" I asked both of them.

"Supporting you." They both said it in unison.

I was really moved. "Thanks. Thanks to both of you."

We moved to one of the large glass-fronted conference rooms in the hall. Mac found the DHS attorney and I gathered Grant and LaReesa. Reese and Dad greeted each other like old friends, and I introduced Reese to Mac, whispering to her that he was one of the two people who had to approve our arrangement. She was polite and friendly.

Mac gave the speech to us that I had given to families about a million times, that this was a Shelter Care Hearing to decide where LaReesa should go, at least temporarily. He had a copy of the court report that I had written last night and emailed him. "You sure you're up for this?" he asked me.

"Absolutely."

He looked at Grant. "And you, Mr. Summerville? Are you up for this?"

Grant shrugged.

He focused on LaReesa. "And you understand that this is a privilege for you? That you have to behave and go to school? If Claire comes to me with any problems, I will have you moved. Do you understand?"

I could see LaReesa struggling and hoped she would remember what I said in the car. I reached over and rubbed her back a couple of times. She glanced at me and I smiled. "I understand, Sir, and I'll behave," she said.

We were called into the courtroom by the bailiff, George. George was hilarious, and loved a good joke, especially about blondes. I didn't have time to tell him one now. He winked at me as we entered, and Judge Myer called us up to the bench. I knew from a previous conversation with LaReesa that her mother's name was LaToya Jones, and I had sent the paperwork down to Tutwiler Prison in Wetumpka last week. She was served by the guards and would have an attorney appointed to her today. Reese and Grant and Mac and I stood in silence as Judge read the report.

It was against policy for me to take LaReesa, and Judge knew it. "This is quite unusual, Miss Conover. You're sure about this?"

"Yes, sir."

"And you, Mr. Summerville?"

"Yes, sir."

"And you, young lady," he addressed LaReesa, "understand you have to behave and go to school and make good grades?"

LaReesa looked uncomfortable and muttered, "I been told."

He announced he was appointing an attorney for Reese's mother, then wrote and signed the order and gave Reese a strong look. "Let me know if there are any problems," he said to me.

"I will, Your Honor."

He dismissed us and we left the courthouse. I said goodbye to Grant and Dad and Mac, then Reese and I headed for Goodwin Middle School in my neighborhood.

"Damn, I got to go today?"

"Yes, ma'am. We are going to get you registered, at least." We pulled up to the school at ten-thirty and met with the seventh and eighth grade counselors and the eighth-grade vice-principal, whose name was Mrs. Roper. It took about two hours to assess what LaReesa had learned and figure out some kind of schedule for her. She'd missed the first half of the eighth grade, and was significantly behind in her knowledge of seventh grade material. The staff pieced together some classes for her and she left with the seventh-grade counselor to find her locker and get her books. LaReesa looked a little nervous and I told her I'd pick her up after school.

I went home and changed into something more comfortable before heading to work. My cell phone rang while I was home. Kirk.

"You busy?" he asked.

"You know me. Always. What's up?"

"I charmed the FBI into to giving me copies of the letters Marcus Freedman has been receiving. Wanna see?"

"Yeah."

"Can you come to my condo?"

"Where's your condo?"

"Beacon Parkway."

"On top of Red Mountain?"

"That's the one."

Red Mountain sits to the south of the city, although "mountain" is a rather optimistic term for the large hill that borders us. The views from the crest are beautiful, though. Kirk gave me quick directions and I was there within a half hour. I was giving up on actually going to work today, considering I told Reese I'd pick her up from school in two hours. Kirk greeted me when I knocked on his door.

"Come on in."

He gave me a brief tour. His unit was nice, two bedrooms decorated in neutral colors with a view of downtown Birmingham that I envied. "You should see it at night," he said. "The view is amazing."

"I'd love to," I said, before I thought.

He chuckled and said, "Allllright."

"I didn't mean that the way it sounded."

"Still hoping maybe someday."

"You have letters?" I asked, desperate to change the subject.

"In my office."

He led me to the bedroom he used as a home office. Framed copies of some of his articles for the *News* hung on the walls. I noted a couple from the cases we had worked on together. He picked up a small stack of papers from his desk.

"I sweet-talked that FBI agent, Deborah Holt, into giving me copies of these. Wasn't too hard to do," he said with a wink. I rolled my eyes at him.

He pulled up a chair for me and we studied the first of the letters. They were handwritten, and most of them were from someone who labeled himself "a Concerned Sitizen" and spelling wasn't his strong suit. It was a lot of racism, and occasionally an outright threat.

Kirk said, "The FBI has identified this genius as one Joseph Robert Gaines. He's called-"

"Lemme guess. Jim Bob?"

"No, better. Joe Bob."

"Really?"

"I know, right? How to make yourself sound like a redneck racist in one easy lesson. He's been sending letters with various levels of threats for some time now. But the thing is, lately the number has been increasing, and the intensity. The Feds got a warrant and picked him up an hour after the bombing. They've got him in jail and have been questioning him for days, but so far he hasn't claimed to have done it, just sings the praises of whoever did."

"Even though the guy who died was white?"

Kirk shrugged. "Logic isn't exactly his strength. He's thinking the bomb will end Dr. Freedman's bid for Mayor."

"Then he doesn't know Marcus."

Kirk passed me another letter by Joe Bob. It looked to have been written by a third grader and started with "You Dam Niger." It went on to say how he needed to drop out of "politicks" and "go back to Afrika."

"Well," I joked, "You know you have to look out for the dam Nigers. Do you really think this asshat has the smarts to build a bomb that can take out a whole building?"

Kirk laughed. "No, not really. But this one…"

He handed me another paper. This one was typed with no misspelled words and all the paragraphs and words were correct. It was a treatise, really, that laid out the points of his argument in clear, concise terms, and ended with a death threat. It scared me more than the first one, by far. It was signed P.W.A.

"The FBI and other law enforcement have not been able to identify who P.W.A. is. They don't know if these are his initials or it stands for something. There is some thought that it might stand for Proud White American. They are working with the Southern Poverty Law Center to go through the known members of hate groups here in our fine state—there's twenty-three, by the way—to see if they can identify him. He's clearly educated and well spoken, likely went to college. Letters of this type began arriving at Marcus Freedman's office about four days after he announced his candidacy for Mayor. Five have been sent so far. No fingerprints or return address, ever. The letter writer could live in Birmingham, or not. He probably lives around here, since he follows the political scene and the letters were mailed in the city."

"That's horrible."

"So far, the threats have been solely directed at Marcus, not at his family, and they were mailed to his office. That's literally all they know."

I was silent for a few minutes, wondering if I needed to move Maddie. If Marcus was getting death threats like this on a regular basis, she might be in an unsafe place. But Marcus and Betty Ann were her family and were falling in love with her. I hated to undo that. I bit my lip.

"What?" Kirk asked.

"I'm just wondering if their granddaughter is safe with them. A bomber took out his office. What if he sets his sights on his home?"

"I guess that's something to consider."

I'd have to chew it over with Mac when I got back to the office. Kirk showed me the other four letters by P.W.A. and it was more of the same. Nearly word for word. At least they weren't increasing in intensity. Kirk said he would stay in contact with the FBI and let me know what came up. I went to the office for an hour before I had to pick up Reese at school.

I checked in with the unit secretary when I arrived and went to Mac's office. He was in conference with another worker from my unit. I let the secretary, Jessica, know my plans for the day and she said she'd let Mac know I wanted to see him. I did a little work at my desk until two thirty and headed back to the middle school.

LaReesa was waiting where I'd instructed this morning with a foul look on her face. *Uh oh*, I thought, as she got in the car. "So how'd it go?"

"There ain't hardly no black kids in this school."

She was right. White flight in decades past had created a nearly all Caucasian community here south of town in the area known as Over the Mountain, while most of the area north of Birmingham was black. "Did you talk to anyone?"

"One girl. She nice. She black. We talked about it. She says you get used to it. I really got to get my hair done. Can I get my hair done?"

"I have no idea where to take you."

"There's a place up near Midfield I been to that ain't too expensive."

"Well, we'll make you an appointment then. How were your classes?"

She shrugged. "They way ahead where I was in Midfield. The teachers was okay."

I sighed with relief. It had actually gone better than I expected. "Do you have homework?"

"A little. In math and science."

"Those are Grant's two favorite subjects."

"Really? Ick."

"I'm just saying if you want someone to help you, he's your guy."

"Okay. Did you order my phone?"

I had left the phone ordering to Grant with instructions on how much to spend. "That's another question for Grant."

I got Reese settled at home with a snack and her homework and set out for Marcus Freedman's home. He lived in an area known as

Crestline which was toward the northeast side of the city. It was one of the more integrated neighborhoods and also held an active gay community. He lived in a pretty ranch-style home built in the seventies. The yard was well-maintained despite being brown for the winter. I complimented it after he let me in.

"Yeah, that's all Betty Ann. She loves to garden."

The interior of the home was just as beautiful as the outside. Betty Ann had really good taste. She emerged from a hallway carrying her granddaughter. I took Maddie from her and went to the sofa where I bounced her on my knee. She was all smiles. I handed her back to Betty Ann and asked to see where the baby was sleeping. Marcus led me back to one of the three bedrooms down the hallway. He turned on the lights in one that contained a crib. The walls were a pretty lavender and there were pinups of actors from several years ago on the walls. A single bed was upended against one wall so the crib could stand in its place. The crib had clean sheets and a soft blanket. Against another wall stood a low dresser with a changing table. I opened the dresser to see lots of warm baby clothes, and plenty of diapers were on the floor next to it. The outlets in the room were baby-proofed. I had seen all I needed to see and said so to Marcus and Betty Ann.

"This was Tameka's room," Betty Ann said, her voice breaking. "I wanted Maddie to have this space, to hopefully feel closer to her, God willing."

I agreed. "I think that's a beautiful idea." We made our way back to the living room. I explained that I had applied for Medicaid for Maddie, which would be approved fairly quickly, and urged them to choose a pediatrician. They gave me a name I was familiar with and I wrote a note to make an appointment. Now came the hard part. I focused on Marcus.

He noticed the look on my face and asked, "What?"

"Have you ever gotten any threatening letters here? Any threats to your home?"

"No, not so far. They've all been mailed to my office. Well, what was my office."

"I need your word that if any threats do come here, you'll call the police, and me."

"Of course. You'd remove Maddie if that happened, though?"

"I'd do everything I could not to, but my primary goal has to be to keep her safe."

"Mine too." Marcus answered. "The FBI has all the letters I've been mailed, and they are looking into who sent them. This house has a very good security system, and I'm keeping an eye out."

"Then I guess that's about all we can do." I stood and told them goodbye, and that I'd be in touch.

Grant and Reese were at the dining room table when I got home. Grant was explaining a pre-algebra problem with a look of serene patience on his face. Reese was animated and agitated.

"No, look, see, you figure this part out first," Grant said.

Reese shoved the notebook to the center of the table. "Why do I gotta know this shit? I don't care what x is."

I interceded. "I think we ought to make plans for dinner, and worry about x later." LaReesa agreed, loudly, with a "Hells yes!"

Grant shot me a look that let me know he was pissed at that statement. "I think we ought to get this done. It's not going to be any easier later."

I went back to the bedroom and began to change clothes, mostly to give us all a bit of time to calm down. Grant followed me and I heard Reese turn on the TV.

"I was trying to help her. You walked in and told her it was okay to quit. How does that help?" he asked.

I closed the bedroom door. "Look, she's had a long day. An emotional day. She is *way* behind in what she needs to know. I'm just saying let's take a break."

"It's not going to be any easier after dinner, when she's more tired."

"I know, and I appreciate your help. But she has no idea why she needs to study this stuff."

"So she can go to high school, maybe college, and have a career."

"But think about life from her perspective for a minute. She's never seen anyone get up and go to a job before. Her grandmother was home, on welfare, raising her grandkids. Her mother...well, she didn't have a job, not a day one anyway. Her aunt sold drugs. A career that requires an education is a completely foreign concept to her. She's never even thought about graduating, much less going to college."

"And we shouldn't expect that of her?"

"Of course, we should, but maybe not on her first day. I don't want her to get overwhelmed and start to hate school. Then we are in real trouble."

I could tell by the look on his face that he didn't agree. We decided to go out to dinner, and LaReesa chose a nearby burger place. I made her promise to put some effort into her homework when we got home. I don't think she did.

The next morning Mac handed me a case at a local elementary school. A boy had shown up with bruises and I was back at the office trying to find him a foster home when my cell phone rang. I didn't recognize the number, but answered it anyway.

A whispered voice asked, "Is this Claire Conover?"

"It is. Can I help you?"

"This is Patricia Alsbrook. I'd like to meet with you."

"Of course, Mrs. Alsbrook. I'm so glad you called."

"It has to be today, at lunch. Can you come to the Pizitz Food Hall?"

"Today? I'm having kind of a busy day, so—"

"Please? I have to do this today." Her voice sounded urgent, and a little scared.

"What time?" I asked.

"Eleven thirty? I'll be seated outside Mo:Mo. You know it?"

"I do, but—"

"Thank you." She hung up.

I glanced at my watch. I had a half hour. Russell was here, but he had ducked up to the records department a few minutes ago. I called him and asked if he could take my bruised little boy for an hour or two and he agreed. He returned to our cubicle as I packed everything up and explained to the boy that I had to run a quick errand and Mr. Russell would be watching him for a while.

The Pizitz Food Hall was a relatively new restaurant center downtown, featuring multiple food "stalls" with cuisines from all over the world, and a really cool bar called The Louis in the middle. The Louis, and the food hall, were named for Louis Pizitz, who owned a chain of dry goods and department stores starting in 1899, with the flagship store here in Birmingham. The Pizitz was walking distance from my office, so rather than pull my car out of the lot, I bundled up in my jacket, walked south a block, and was soon there.

The food hall was on the first floor of the renovated former Pizitz Department store, which had been built in 1923. The upper floors had been converted to apartments and offices, and the ground floor featured everything from Japanese to Mexican to Israeli food. The stall Patricia Alsbrook had mentioned served Nepalese and Vietnamese food.

The whole floor was getting a little crowded as the lunch hour approached. I scanned the crowd and spotted Patricia Alsbrook seated at a bar height table at Mo:Mo. She wore a fleece-lined coat with a hood that nearly hid her head it was so big on her. Ronald

Cushman, Alsbrook's security guy, was with her. His hulking form stood behind her, surveying the crowd. I approached them.

"Mrs. Alsbrook?"

A steaming bowl of dumplings sat in front of her. She hadn't touched it yet. She gestured to a seat across from her. "Patricia, please. I'm sorry for such short notice. I told my husband I was having lunch here with a girlfriend. He installed an app on my phone that tracks where I go, so it had to be here."

"Can't you leave the phone at home?"

"Oh, no. That would be a bad idea."

Ronald remained standing, still on the lookout for something. I encouraged Patricia to finish her lunch but she pushed it to the middle of the table. "He checks my credit and debit cards daily, so I had to order something."

"Patricia, is he…hurting you? Hitting you?"

"He has for years." She looked at the table as her eyes filled with tears. "He has a bit of a violent temper, you see. Sweet Ronald here, he's had to step in a couple—a few—times."

I glanced at Ronald, who shrugged.

"You know there are shelters? For women in these kinds of relationships? They can keep you safe."

"I couldn't go to a shelter. Oh, no. Jason was going to help. He was getting ready to get me out. Then Tameka died, and he had to take Maddie full time. He was still trying to help, but it just got delayed. I don't know how I'd get out now that Jason is…" Tears overflowed and Sweet Ronald laid a gentle hand on her shoulder. "I feel so guilty for raising him in that house. We should have left when he was a baby. He witnessed so much." She dug a tissue out of her purse and wiped her eyes. "How's Maddie?" she asked.

"She's with the Freedmans and doing great. Would you like to see her?"

"James would never allow that."

My heart ached for this poor woman who was so trapped. "I could get you some pictures," I ventured.

"How would I get them? He goes through any mail I get, and checks my phone and email daily."

"I could print them. Give me some time and I'll figure it out."

Ronald leaned down close to Patricia's ear. "He's here," he said softly.

The panic rose on Patricia's face instantly. "Oh my God. He's here. He's here---we have to go. I'm so sorry."

Ronald reached down and put a hand on her shoulder. "Stay

calm. I've scouted the exits and have a way out."

I had a sudden insight. "Are you a veteran?" I asked Ronald.

"Yes, ma'am. Special Forces. Many years ago."

"I'll go talk to him," I said, "give you a few minutes head start."

She was shaking. "Please don't tell him we talked. Please don't tell him you saw me."

"I won't. Go now. I'll be in touch."

I stood and walked in the direction Ronald pointed. James was in a different suit today, navy blue, with polka-dotted tie neatly knotted and the pants pressed. He was shaking hands with someone as I approached. I waited until they finished their brief conversation, subtly looking over my shoulder for Patricia and Ronald, who had disappeared.

Mr. Alsbrook spotted me. "Miss Conover? Funny meeting you here."

"My office is nearby. I came over to grab a bahn mi." I nodded to Mo:Mo, where I'd been moments before. "Your granddaughter is doing well. Have you given any more thought to—"

"No! I meant it when I said I don't consider Jason's mistake to be my family. Have you seen my wife?" He looked around the room.

"No, is she here? I haven't seen her. Well, I'm going to go grab my sandwich. Nice to see you," I lied. "Please feel free to call me if you change your mind." I offered him a business card. He ignored it and I slipped it back in my purse.

Patricia had vanished with Ronald like magic. I walked away and saw James checking his phone, probably tracking her like she had said. I hoped she was in her car and on her way home. I bought a sandwich and walked back to the office, thanking Russell for his help by handing him the sandwich.

"Thank you! Oh my God, these are wonderful. You sure you don't want it?"

"I'm sure."

I got ahold of my little client's grandparents in St. Clair County, and they agreed he could stay with them for a few weeks. It was an hour drive there and an hour back, and I didn't pull into my drive until nearly eight o'clock that night. Grant's van was parked at the curb.

I used my key to let myself into the house through the carport. I entered the house into the kitchen and was greeted with a squealing, screaming LaReesa.

Chapter Ten

"It's here! It's here! Isn't it awesome? Selfie!" LaReesa threw her arm around my shoulders and a flash went off in my face.

"Wonderful," I muttered as Grant planted a kiss on my cheek.

"It's a Samsung Galaxy. Isn't it cool?" Reese squealed.

I put my stuff down in my bedroom and went to hear all about the "super cool" phone. "That was fast." I said to Grant.

"I found one refurbished. Didn't take long to get here at all. I plugged her into your plan."

"Thanks," I answered, thumbing through the pile of mail on the kitchen counter.

"I made a salad and some grilled chicken for dinner. It's in the fridge if you're hungry."

"Yeah, thanks. It's been a very long day."

LaReesa was typing madly with her thumbs on the phone in her hand. "This is so cool."

"Be sure to thank Grant."

"Oh, I did."

Grant nodded. "Many times."

"Did you do your homework?"

"I will in a bit."

I held out my hand. "Give me the phone."

The expression on her face looked like I had just declared martial law. "Why?"

"I'm going to take that phone for three hours every evening so you can do your homework."

She slapped the phone into my hand so hard it stung. "That ain't fuckin' fair."

"You want to try for twenty-four hours without it?"

"You in a mood today."

"Go do your homework."

I ate some salad while listening to Reece grumble under her breath about how life wasn't fair, then went to bed. Sleep was elusive, and I found myself thinking about Marcus and the bombing again. Going over it again and again in my head and wondering why. Why someone would hate him so much they'd want to kill him. Wondering about little Maddie and her daddy and why they were the victims of this. Did I need to put her in a different home, in foster care? The ceiling in the bedroom held no answers. Unless…

I sat up and checked the clock on my phone. It read nine thirty-six. I dialed Kirk's number.

"Hello?" He sounded sleepy.

"Did I wake you? I'm sorry."

"No, no. I'm up. What's going on?"

"What if Marcus wasn't supposed to be killed? What if the bomb was meant for Jason all along?"

"Okay, and?"

"I mean, do you think the cops are looking into that?"

"I don't know. What makes you think someone would want Jason dead?"

Motive. Yeah. That was important. I thought for a second. "How many Mourned Miners did you say there were?"

"Thirty-three, in the last twenty years."

"Maybe that's it. Maybe it's a...a revenge killing. Like you killed my son, now I'm going to kill yours. Do you know anything about the miners?"

"Not much, but I know someone who does. I'll call her and set up a meeting."

"For tomorrow?"

"Yes, dear."

"Kirk--"

"I know. I'll text you in a bit." He hung up.

I lay down again, mind racing. I was dying to call the FBI to see if they had thought about my theory. Not that they were answering the phone at this time of night.

Ten minutes later, my phone pinged. Kirk. The text said, "Meeting set up at ten tomorrow morning. I'll pick you up in the lot at nine-fifteen."

"Thx" I texted back. Now I was too excited to sleep, so I went to check on Reese. She was at the dining room table, finishing the last of a science study guide. Grant was watching TV.

"How's it going?" I asked.

"Not bad. One more to do. Grant helped me with the math. It's awful."

I laughed. I'd had the same opinion of math in middle school, but I didn't tell her that. Back in my bedroom, I got my laptop, booted it up, and Googled the Mourned Miners. They had a very basic website, not much more than a series of photographs of deceased men and a phone number offering help to anyone who had lost a loved one in tragic mine accidents in Alabama. There was a short paragraph about mining accidents. They were a lot more common than I would have thought.

Grant came to bed at ten-thirty and I put the laptop away. The next morning, I was at work by seven-thirty and at nine-fifteen was impatiently pacing in the parking lot. Kirk roared up in his Infinity right on time.

"You're full of pep today."

I fastened my seatbelt. "I'm just anxious to talk to this woman. What's her name?"

"Dana Burke. She founded the Mourned Miners after her son was killed."

"Where are we going?"

"Calera."

Calera was a small town in Shelby County, the next county south of Birmingham. It had been a growing suburb of Birmingham for years, drawing people because of its good school system and affordable housing. Kirk raced down the interstate as I stared out of the window at passing cars.

Forty minutes later we pulled into a campground. RV's lined the park which was shaded with tall pine trees. A small building sat in the center. I wondered what it was. The office, maybe. Kirk drove around the park and pulled into lot 32. The camper looked as if it had been there for a while. A wooden deck had been added to the front and was covered with a handcrafted metal roof. Kirk knocked on the small door.

It was opened by a grey-haired woman about my height. She wore square-framed glasses and her stocky body was dressed neatly in a tunic and tights.

"Are you Dana?" Kirk asked.

"I am. Please come in."

The RV was cozy and cute, neatly decorated in shades of red and yellow. A small dog, brown in color, sat on a chair by the door. He barked loudly at us as we entered. "That's Zeus, just ignore him. Have a seat."

Kirk and I sat shoulder to shoulder on a small sofa. Dana offered us water, which we declined. She picked up the dog and sat with him in her lap as I studied a small collection of photographs on a window sill behind her. There were several photos of a lanky young man with sharp features and spiky hair. Small candles were lit amongst the framed pictures. "Is that your son?" I asked.

She smiled. "That's Benjamin junior. He was killed in the explosion at the Warm Creek mine down here."

"I'm so sorry."

Tears filled Dana's eyes. "His daddy was a miner, too. We're divorced now. We never could get back on track after B.B. was killed. B.B. was his nickname, for Ben Burke. The only thing B.B. ever wanted to do was work in the mines like his grandpa and his daddy. He was twenty-four when he was killed."

My eyes went back to the series of photos. "Where's his father now? Does he live here?"

"No, he lives in Florida. Just south of Jacksonville. Lives on a boat and does maintenance around the marina to pay his rent."

So good chance he wasn't a suspect, I thought. Dana reached to her left, to the counter next to the tiny stove, and retrieved a stack of papers. "Mr. Mahoney asked for a list of the miner's families killed in Alabama that we've worked with, especially those who are younger. I pulled out most of the names of the older miners." she explained, handing the papers to Kirk. "That's all of them, but there's more that we haven't helped. And more we couldn't afford to help."

"You heard about James Alsbrook's son being killed? In the bombing?" I asked.

Her glance went to the photos again. "I wouldn't wish this on anybody. I'm so sorry. Mr. Alsbrook donated money to our organization."

"Ten thousand dollars, I heard," Kirk said.

She shrugged. "Every little bit helps."

Little being the operative word, I thought.

Kirk continued, "Do you still talk to the families? Of the victims?"

"There were five miners killed with B.B. I still talk to a lot of those women, the mothers and the wives, especially when the anniversary of the accident rolls around on September sixteenth. It helps, on the bad days."

"What happened?" I asked.

"They were using old equipment that wasn't in good shape. Best the investigators can tell, one of the lamps sparked, setting off a methane explosion. My son's group was closest and all of them were killed instantly. Another miner died later from his burns, at the hospital."

"I'm so sorry."

"Methane and other explosions are one of the most common causes of accidents in the mines. There're a lot of people killed in China every year, and about sixty to seventy miners die every year in the U.S."

"And the Mourned Miners helps with funeral costs? That kind of thing?"

Dana nodded. "Sometimes we just pay the bills for a month, until the family can figure out what they are going to do. The miners are often the main breadwinner in the family, so their death really hurts financially. We try to encourage everyone to get life insurance, but some can't afford it."

"Where do you get your funds?" I asked.

"A few times a year we have fundraisers. Nothing fancy, mind you. Like a car wash. Or a yard sale."

Kirk stated, "I'm going to write an article for the News about your organization. Where can my readers send donations?" "Oh, that would be wonderful!" Dana exclaimed. "My address is on the forms I gave you. I would really appreciate that."

Kirk and I stood in the cramped space and said goodbye. Kirk asked for a picture of B.B. and he swore to return it as soon as he could. She handed the photo over slowly, her eyes lingering on the image for a moment. My heart ached for this woman and her loss. All that was left were these photos. I got a little choked up once I was back in the car with Kirk. He noticed.

"You okay?"

"Yeah, it's just so sad. I really admire what Dana has done, taking her tragedy and turning it around to help others."

"You are such a big-hearted person."

I shrugged. "I'm just a humanist, that's all."

"Can you come over this evening? We can start going through this list and doing some research."

"Let me check with Grant but I probably can."

Kirk dropped me off at work and I called Grant at the shop and explained that I had to work tonight and could he please feed Reese and make sure her homework got done? He agreed.

I worked until five, then headed up the mountain to Kirk's condo. I brought my laptop, thinking we may need some extra computer power for this research. He answered the door with a glass of white wine in his hand, which he handed to me.

I laughed, "Thanks."

"Thought you might need it. I've got us set up at the dining room table."

The table was just off the kitchen, a modern glass-topped round table surrounded by four chairs. Kirk's laptop was set up there, along with a notebook and pen and the small stack of papers he'd gotten from Dana.

"I've already gone through the list once. There're sixteen names on it, since Dana pulled out the ones who are older. I'm researching whether there are others killed recently that the Mourned Miners didn't help. She seems to have made contact at least with all of them, even the few she didn't help."

"What can I do?"

"Research the names. Try to find obituaries online and see where the parents live. Then we'll go from there."

I took the top list off the stack of papers. Dana had arranged it in columns, with the deceased's name and age, then the name of the mine, then the date of death, and a family member's name. As Kirk had said, there were sixteen in total. I scanned down, reading all the names until one caught my eye. I felt the room shift and my stomach sank to the floor.

My breath caught and Kirk heard it. "What?"

"Chad Davenport."

"What about him?"

"He was killed a couple years ago in a mining accident. I knew him."

My mind pictured him how he was when I met him. He was one of my first cases. He was a small kid, then eleven years old, red hair that would never lie down and a gap-toothed smile. Russell had nicknamed him Opie. I did an investigation and then went to the house with a police officer to take Chad and his sister into foster care—oh, somewhere around ten years ago. His elementary school had initially reported him to us. Apparently, Chad was showing up to school hungry, and was begging for change from other kids to buy something to eat in the cafeteria.

We got out to the house in north Jefferson County and the officer arrested their schizophrenic father after he reached for a gun and threatened to kill us all. His sister Caitlynn, aged eight, sobbed the whole way to my office. Chad was resigned and quiet, like he knew it was coming. His dad had been committed to a mental institution and I had transferred the case to another social worker. They aged out of the foster care system and I'd lost track of what happened to them after that. As I remembered, they'd been good foster kids with no blown placements and not a lot of social or educational problems.

Kirk interrupted my thoughts. "How'd you know him?"

"He was a foster kid. His Dad is nuts. Like, seriously very mentally ill."

"Like someone who could blow up a building?"

"I don't know. The man I knew, his name is Dwayne, was so schizophrenic he couldn't function. His wife, Chad's mother, vanished years ago. She just took off after the daughter was born."

"Nice." Kirk said. "Do you have his address? We should go talk to Dwayne."

"Oh no, I don't think so. He pulled a gun on me and a cop the last time I saw him. I don't think he functions well enough to build a bomb. And if he remembers me, he may very well try to kill me."

I focused back on the list. There suddenly seemed to be a lot of names. Glenn Coyne. Timothy Kramer. Ronnie Parks. Douglas McGriff. I looked up their obituaries and wrote down names of grieving mothers and fathers. I wondered about Chad. Who had buried him? Who had grieved him?

"You okay?"

"Yeah just a little shocked at the news about Chad. He was a really sweet kid. He had a chaotic, short life."

"I'll make us some coffee." Kirk stood and went to the kitchen. I rose and followed him, watching him gather the filter and grind the beans. He wore a white t-shirt and loose, gray, pajama-like pants that looked good on him.

He turned and caught me checking him out. I looked at the floor. He started the coffee machine and walked to where I stood. Kirk reached out and grasped my face, gently. His eyes were an intense blue.

I was so tired of abused kids. I was tired of the instability these little kids had to deal with on a daily basis. Little Michael Hennessy, who had died last year. Samantha, also from last year. Chad. His sister, Caitlynn. LaReesa.

Kirk leaned in.

My whole body ached. I couldn't remember the last time I had a day off.

His lips met mine. It started as a soft kiss, then grew more intense when I didn't pull away.

I was tired.

And he was such a good kisser.

I needed to leave.

I didn't.

Chapter Eleven

We ended up in Kirk's bed, eventually. After it was all over, I lay there, the guilt of what I'd done lying on me like the heavy blanket. I checked my phone. It was seven thirty p.m. I crawled out of the bed and began to get dressed.

"You're leaving?"

"I have to go. Tomorrow is a school day and I'm sure my foster kid has homework. And I have work to do."

"Can I call you tomorrow?"

"I don't think so. This was a huge mistake, and I have to figure out how I'm going to handle this."

"You going to tell Grant?"

"No! No way. I don't know. Maybe. I have to go." I gathered all my stuff quickly and walked to my car. I sat there for a few minutes, fighting back tears as I considered what to do next.

I needed to go home, but I didn't want to. Grant would take one look at my face and know something was up. I cranked the car and headed down the mountain.

The sex had been amazing. Kirk knew what he was doing and I'd completely gotten lost in the moment, experiencing nothing but the sensations of his touch all over my body.

But it could never happen again. Never. I drove to I-65 and headed south. I hated myself. I had such a good thing going with Grant. Why had I allowed this to happen? I drove past my exit and continued south.

Where was I going? What was I going to do? I exited the interstate in the town of Pelham and headed east. In twenty minutes, I parked in a driveway and checked the clock on my dashboard. It was eight fifteen. I hoped I wasn't going to interrupt the kids' bedtime routine. I walked up to the door and knocked softly.

Toby answered the door and saw it was me and said, "Hey. Roy's bathing the kids. Hang on."

I waited in the neat living room while Toby went and fetched Royanne. Royanne Fayard was my best friend, and had been since fifth grade. She and her teddy-bear husband had three kids, who were now three, five, and seven. She emerged from the hallway, drying her hands on a towel.

"Hey, what's up?" she asked.

"You got a second to talk? Can we go outside?"

"It's forty degrees outside."

"Please?"

We went out to her driveway after she threw on an extra-large sweatshirt of Toby's. "What's going on?"

"I cheated on Grant. I hate myself and I don't know what I'm going to do."

"What? Cheated on him? With who? Just a one-night hookup? That doesn't sound like you."

"It was with Kirk Mahoney."

"The hottie from the newspaper? Oh my God. Was it good?"

"Royanne--"

"Okay, you can save the details. When did this happen?"

I glanced at my watch. "About two hours ago."

She laughed. "So you haven't told Grant, I take it."

"I haven't even been home yet. I needed to talk about this with somebody because I feel so awful. He's going to take one look at me and know something's up."

"No, he's not. And don't tell him. Not if you want to save this relationship. Just act like nothing happened and it will be fine."

"You think so?"

"As long as you don't say anything. The guilt will get better. As long as Grant doesn't find out, y'all will be fine."

I hugged her. "Thanks. I feel so awful."

"Come in the house and say hi to the kids and wash your face."

I made my way to the hall bathroom, which was also the kids' bathroom. The walls were a pretty powder blue and it was decorated with cartoon frogs—frogs on the shower curtain and silly little frogs on the light green towels. I splashed my face with cool water and wiped it on the silly frog towel. I checked myself in the mirror, noting the bags under my eyes and my ruffled hair. I dug a hairbrush out of my purse and neatened it up. I took a deep breath and began to feel like I could handle going home.

Richard, Royanne's five-year-old, greeted me in the hallway with a huge hug around my waist. I knelt down and returned it. "Wanna see my train?"

"Sure, buddy."

He took me back to his bedroom, where a large track and a toy train sat on the floor. I sat down beside it as he pushed the three chunky, wooden train cars around the track, narrating the journey with a "chugga chugga chugga woot woot."

Royanne smiled at us from the door. "He's a little train obsessed these days. I don't think there's an episode of Thomas the Tank Engine we haven't seen."

I smiled back. Alicia, aged seven and the oldest of Royanne's kids, walked in carrying a Judy Blume book, *Tales of a Fourth Grade Nothing*. "Mama, it's story time."

"Maybe Aunt Claire will read you a Chapter One."

I checked my watch. Eight forty-five. I had to go, and regretfully stated this to the kids. I hugged Roy again and made my way home. I parked in the carport at nine-fifteen, wondering why Grant's van wasn't there.

I heard LaReesa laugh as I walked into the living room. She was sitting on the lap of a young black man who looked to be about twenty. Or older. His eyes were bloodshot red. Another young man sat across the room, a mellow look on his face, his eyes also red. All my guilt immediately turned to burning anger. I took a couple of deep breaths and moved to where Reese could see me. The look on her face was almost comical. Her eyebrows shot up in surprise as she leapt off the boy's—man's—lap. I felt my temper rising further.

"Where's Grant?"

"He left. He had an emergency. He tried to call you but you din' pick up."

"Who are your friends?"

"Oh, dis T-bone," she said, nodding to the man on whose lap she'd been sitting. "And that's K-dog."

I didn't bother to ask for real names. "Well, gentlemen, this *eighth grader* has school tomorrow, so it's time to go home."

The guys didn't look very surprised at the eighth-grade news. I palmed my cell phone in case I needed help, but I didn't. The guys left quietly out the front door as LaReesa turned on me.

"So now I can't even have friends! Fuck!"

"Those guys are adults and you're baked."

"Aw, it was jus' a little weed. Chill, ain't no big thing. We din' even smoke it in the house."

"Reese! It is a big thing. It's illegal, at least for now, and it's against my rules. Is that understood? Never. Again."

"But—"

"Do you remember what Judge Myer said to you? What you had to do if you want to stay here?"

My friend Danessa Brown taught the required classes for future foster parents every Tuesday evening. I sat in sometimes, to help explain how investigations went. Her voice echoed in my head. *Don't threaten the kids with removal, no matter how bad the behavior is. They are going to test their limits. Their lives are unpredictable enough without the threat of being homeless. And* then if you don't have them removed, they learn you make empty threats. Be a source of strength.

"You kickin' me out?" LaReesa asked. At least she had the sense to look a little scared.

"Reese, if you can't get it together—"

Grant walked in the door from the carport. "What's going on?"

I answered him, "I got home from work and she had two men here. They were in their twenties, and they were all stoned."

"Stoned," LaReesa said, mocking me. "Ha ha. I'm hungry."

Grant laughed, which really didn't help the situation. I went back to our room and Grant followed. Reese began to rummage in the kitchen for snacks.

I turned to him. "Laughing doesn't help the situation."

"I know. I'm sorry, but it was funny."

"She was sitting on the lap of one of the men when I got here. I'm terrified she's going to go down the same road as her mother."

"She may very well. But like you said, let's not expect that."

"I'm going to take a bath. A very long, hot bath."

"I had a client who had a server crash. I'm sorry, I had to go. I tried to reach you when I left."

"I didn't have my phone on me." *It was in the bottom of my purse while I was screwing Kirk.*

"Have you eaten? I can make some sandwiches while you're in the bath."

The guilt in my gut twisted and felt like a stab. "That would be wonderful."

"Then I better get in there before she eats everything." I smiled, and Grant left for the kitchen. I stripped my clothes off and took a long bubble bath, scrubbing my skin in the hopes it would wash away the guilt. Afterwards, I put on warm flannel pajamas and joined them in the kitchen. Grant had made gooey grilled cheese sandwiches and Reese was finishing one when I walked in. "That's her third," he said as he passed the plate to me.

"Then it's her bedtime," I said, grabbing a sandwich.

Reese didn't protest as she left the kitchen, saying a sleepy "G'night" over her shoulder. I was sure she hadn't done her homework and didn't want to push it when she was high. I knew her grades were going to suffer and I figured I'd deal with that later.

Grant walked over and pulled me into a hug. "You look tired," he said.

"Thanks!"

"Sorry. I meant radiant. You look radiant."

"It was a long day at work."

"Do you ever have a not-long day?"

"Good point," I said through a yawn. "Saving the world takes energy. I'm going to bed."

"What about Reese? What's her consequence for this?"

"I'm taking that damn phone for a week. At least."

"Better sneak in and get it now before she hides it."

"Another good point." Grant followed me to Reese's room. She was sound asleep already, lying on her back and snoring softly. I unplugged the phone from the cord on her nightstand and we went to our room.

"Can we see what's on this?" I asked.

"Sure," he reached out and I handed him the phone.

He typed on the screen. "She's changed the password, even though I told her not to."

We went to the office where he retrieved a small, looped wire. He took the phone out of its glittery case and used the wire to pop open the slot where the SIM card sat. He placed the card in a USB adapter and plugged that into a laptop. He sat in front of the machine and began to type.

"This may take a while. I'm going to lock the phone in my lock box in here and search this card tomorrow."

"Okay, thanks." I leaned down and kissed him on the cheek. "I'm going to bed."

He hugged my waist. "I'll be right in."

I lay in bed and tried to sleep, but the guilt from earlier crept in too easily. Grant came to bed and I pretended to be asleep. I couldn't face any intimacy with him.

Not tonight.

Chapter Twelve

When I woke up the next morning, LaReesa was yelling at Grant, and he was handling it with his typical, quiet calmness.

"Where the *fuck* is my phone?!" she was demanding.

He answered, "I believe you have lost the privilege of having a phone by inviting older guys over here and smoking weed. That's just my guess."

"That ain't your call!"

"No, it's mine." I stated, entering the kitchen where they were talking. I poured myself a mug of black coffee and faced her.

"This ain't fair!"

"Did you really think I would be okay with you having older men over and smoking marijuana?" She mocked me again. *"Did you really think I would be okay with you having older men over and smoking marijuana?* God, you are so old."

"I am mature, LaReesa. Which is what I'm trying to get you to be. You have school today, you know."

"I know, I'm gonna go get ready. I was gonna use my *phone* to schedule my hair appointment."

"Tell me the name of the place and I'll call them today."

"They called Sophistication and they in Powderly." Powderly was an area near Midfield, where Reese had lived with her grandmother, and her mother before she'd gone to prison.

"Okay."

"An' I want braids. Long braids, if it ain't too much."

"Okay." She left the kitchen and within moments we heard the shower begin.

"Whew," I said to Grant, walking to him and putting my arms around his waist.

He kissed me on the top of my head. "I tried to tell you she's a handful."

I took a deep breath. "She is starting a new life, with a level of responsibility she has never had before."

"Let's keep telling ourselves that."

I got ready for work and left after dropping Reese off at school. She didn't speak to me the entire time we were in the car, and left me in carpool after slamming the door without so much as a goodbye. "Have a great day!" I called after her.

As I arrived at work, my phone rang. Kirk. I picked up.

"Hello, gorgeous." For some reason that statement made my

skin crawl. "How are you?"

"Hi, Kirk. What's up?"

"I wanted to call and say how much I enjoyed last night. Are we okay?"

"I don't want to talk about it. I don't ever want to talk about it and it will never happen again. Understood?"

"Sure." His tone changed from flirty to serious. "Absolutely. I'm going out to talk to Dwayne Davenport today. I wanted to see if you would come along."

"I told you he pulled a gun on me, right?"

"We'll be careful, I promise."

"Why? Why are you talking to him? To try to find Jason's killer?"

"Yes, that, and I'm doing an article on James Alsbrook. How his mines have accidents and how it affects the community."

"You want to take him down."

"That would be a glorious side effect."

"I hope you have a lot of lawyers."

"Ha! That's what my editor said. Do you want to come, or not?"

"I've got appointments all afternoon and then I have to pick up LaReesa at school."

"I'm going at lunchtime. LaReesa's your foster kid?"

"Yes."

"I'll pick you up at noon?" He left it with a bit of a question.

"I'll be in the back lot."

"See you then." He hung up.

I shouldn't do this, I thought. I needed to distance myself from him and work on things with Grant. The guilt about yesterday kicked in again and I quietly crept up to my cubicle. Russell was there, unpacking his briefcase. "Hey."

"Hey."

"You alright?" he asked.

"Yeah. Why?"

"You seem a little down about something. Bad case?"

"No, I'm fine. How are you?"

"Girl, I'm hungover. I went out last night and met the cutest guy. We talked and drank till midnight. I got his number and I think we are going to get together this weekend."

Russell had been in a relationship that dissolved last summer, so I was glad he had met someone. We talked as we worked on paperwork and at noon, I met Kirk in the lot.

I didn't look at him as I entered his silver Infiniti. I couldn't bring myself to make eye contact with him as he greeted me and we headed for the suburb of Pinson, north of Birmingham, where Mr. Davenport lived.

"You mad at me?" he asked.

"I'm mad at myself. Really mad."

"So you didn't tell Grant?"

"Of course not! I love him, and I don't want to lose him."

"Then it's our secret."

"Can we talk about something else?"

"What can you tell me about Dwayne Davenport?"

I shrugged. "All this is off the record, of course. He has paranoid schizophrenia. He lost his kids ten years ago and was eventually committed to the State psych hospital, Bryce, in Tuscaloosa. I don't know how long he stayed there, but it was a few months, maybe a year. I don't know, maybe even two. He never got his kids back. Never tried, as far as I know. The kids were raised by foster parents and aged out of the system."

"You said he pulled a gun on you?"

"He wasn't really willing to let his kids go."

"What about their mother?"

"She disappeared after Caitlynn was born. We made an attempt to find her, then the Court did, but no luck. She just vanished. I don't know where she is."

We pulled into the neighborhood in Pinson. It looked a lot like it did ten years ago. The houses were split levels built in the nineteen-sixties and seventies. Dwayne Davenport's house looked exactly as it had ten years ago, but was much more worn. It needed to be painted badly. The dark green paint was cracked and chipping in many places. The door to the mailbox hung from one hinge. Kirk parked in the driveway, then we made our way to the faded green front door. I was a little nervous and found myself gripping my cell phone tightly.

"Relax," Kirk whispered. I nodded as he knocked.

"Come in."

Dwayne looked much, much older than the last time I'd seen him. He'd gained a lot of weight that sat around his middle and in his face. It was scruffy, like he hadn't shaved in a few days. He sat in a threadbare recliner that I remembered from my last visit. His stare was far away, distant, like he wasn't really here.

Kirk introduced himself. Dwayne stood up and shook his hand. His mouth twitched, almost puckering, and his eyes blinked too often. It looked strange, and I could see Kirk reacting to it. I introduced myself, scanning the room for guns, and was relieved to see there weren't any visible. We sat down, and I asked Dwayne if he remembered me.

"No, sorry."

"That's okay. I was sorry to hear about Chad."

"He was killed in the Green Valley mine. They had an explosion."

"Do you know what happened?" Kirk asked.

"They said they was usin' explosives that was old. Too old. What was the word they used? Degenerated. Thas' it."

Kirk asked, "Did you get any compensation for his death? Any money from the mine?"

"Naw. There was this one woman, forgot her name, that came out. She helped with the funeral since Chad didn't have no life insurance. She was nice. Her boy was killed a few years ago in the mines, too."

Dana, I thought. "How is Caitlynn?" I asked.

His affect didn't change at the mention of her name, still the same far-away look. "She comes over every night and brings me food. She's married and has a little baby. Little J.T. He's real cute. He's six months old. I'm on disability now, so I don't do much. She lives nearby and takes care of me."

"She's what, eighteen now?" I asked.

"Bout to turn nineteen."

Not even nineteen and has a six-month-old, I thought. And a mentally ill father to take care of. Not an easy life. My mind began to list resources for her as Kirk thanked Dwayne for his time.

"Why y'all out here?" he asked. "What we talking about this for?"

Kirk answered. "There's a man who owns the mine where Chad was killed. His mines have more mining accidents than any of them here. I want to expose that in the newspaper, and tell Chad's story."

"And I just wanted to express my condolences about Chad," I added. "He was a very bright little boy."

Dwayne focused on me, and I could see him trying hard to concentrate. "Oh, yeah, I remember you now. You with DHS."

I felt my stomach tighten with a touch of fear. "Yes, sir."

"I pulled a rifle on you."

"Yes, sir."

"Sorry 'bout that. They came and took all my guns away while

I was in Bryce Hospital. Said I wasn't stable enough to own them. Guess they right."

"Please tell Caitlynn I said hello."

Kirk and I said our goodbyes and headed back to the city.

"What was all that thing with his face? He kept twitching."

"That's called Tardive Dyskinesia. It's caused by the antipsychotic meds he's been on for years."

"Can't they treat it?"

"There are meds to help control it. I don't know why he's not on them."

"I'm going to call Glenn Coyne's family next. Wanna come with?"

"Why? I don't know them or have any reason to speak to them."

"I appreciate your insight. Like noticing what was going on with Mrs. Alsbrook, her wearing baggy clothes and stuff. I totally missed that. Come with me, please?"

"When?"

"Tomorrow? When are you free?"

I pulled up my calendar on my phone. Tomorrow was a court review in the morning, but I was free in the afternoon until three thirty and told Kirk so. We decided on one o'clock and he dropped me off at work.

My appointments in the afternoon went very well and I had two cases that I could close. I was in a good mood as I waited for Reese at school. She walked toward the carpool line while talking to a black girl about her age. They said goodbye and Reese got in the car.

"You speaking to me now?" I asked. "Who's your friend?"

She shrugged. "That's Sharonda. She really nice. She ask me to come over to her house and spend the night on Saturday. Can I go?"

"If your homework is done and you behave."

"Did you call about my hair?"

"I haven't had a chance yet but we can when we get home."

I got a smile for that statement and make good on my word when we reached the house. She had an appointment for ten a.m. on Saturday. I asked LaReesa to let Sharonda know I'd need to talk to her mother before she could make plans for Saturday night.

"But I don't have my phone. How my s'posed to talk to her if I can't text?"

"When you get to school tomorrow, get her mom's phone number."

"So ol' school."

"Hmm, I don't know how we made it to the twenty-first century."

She stormed off to the dining room to do her homework as I did updates and a court report in the office. I'd have to warn Sharonda's mother, bless her heart, about LaReesa's temper and have her keep a close watch on the both of them. I hoped Sharonda wasn't going to be a bad influence, or vice versa. That was all I needed.

Grant came home and met me in the office. He closed the door behind him and offered to continue to look at the contents on Reese's phone. I kept working while he detected the information on her phone using his laptop. After some time, he called me over. I peered over his shoulder as he pointed out her contacts and her texts.

"There's mostly boys," he said, pointing to her contacts.

"Or men. Can you delete them?"

"I can, but she'll just get them again."

"But it may slow her down, anyway."

"I'm going to check her search history." He typed for a while. "It looks like it's mostly hairstyles and clothes."

"Good. That's appropriate."

"Uh oh."

"What?"

"Here's 'how old do you have to be to buy condoms'"

"Oh, no. I need to make her an appointment to get checked for STDs and maybe get her some birth control."

"Couldn't hurt, for sure. I'll lock this back in the box for you if you like."

"Thanks."

"You okay?"

"Sure, why?"

"I just feel like you are a little bothered. Distant. Are we okay?"

I cheated on you. I had sex with Kirk Mahoney. "Sure. Everything's fine."

Even I didn't believe it.

Chapter Thirteen

The next day was Friday, and I had a court review that went fairly badly. The parents in that case did not get custody back as they had hoped, and it took me a solid twenty minutes to calm everybody down after the judge dismissed us. I was late getting back to the office. I made a quick call to my gynecologist and made an appointment for LaReesa for the next week, and also called the pediatrician for little Maddie Freedman and made her an appointment for next Tuesday.

I met Kirk at one as we agreed. We sped off to Rock Creek, an area of town northwest of Birmingham, close to the suburb of Hueytown. It was a rural community of about a thousand residents. The Coynes lived on several acres, in a small house that faced the road with an enormous metal shop in the back. I wondered if Mr. Coyne was a mechanic since the shop was large enough to be a garage. Kirk knocked on the front door. It was opened by a small, middle-aged woman with long, graying hair. She looked at us inquisitively.

"Mrs. Julia Coyne?" Kirk asked.

"Yes?"

"My name is Kirk Mahoney, and I'm a reporter with the *News*. I'm doing a story on James Alsbrook and I'd like to talk to you and your husband about your son."

"He's dead."

"Yes, I know. Can we talk about him? I'd like to talk about Mr. Alsbrook's role in your son's death."

I could see she was becoming agitated, and her eyes were filling with tears. I stepped in. "Mrs. Coyne, we were so sorry to hear about your son. I'm sure this must be painful. We don't want to hurt you, and we don't have to talk about anything that makes you uncomfortable."

Kirk shot me an annoyed look. "Of course, we don't. Is your husband home? Mr. Coyne?"

"He's back in the shop, getting organized after the holiday."

"The holiday?" Kirk asked.

"New Year's Day. We own Coyne's Fireworks. You might have seen our trailers around town around the holidays?"

"Oh, yeah," I said. "They've been around since I was a kid." Fireworks were illegal in all the incorporated towns in Alabama, but Dad would take me and Chris to the unincorporated areas of the County to buy them, and we would set them off in the driveway. As long as people were careful, law enforcement looked the other way.

"Can we meet your husband? Wendell? Is that right?" Kirk asked.

She nodded. "Come on through the house. My husband's name is Wendell but everybody calls him Flip."

"Flip Coyne, that's cute." I said.

She led us through the neat house to a nicely furnished deck out back. Three steps led down to the yard and we walked across it to the enormous building. A metal sign that read "Coyne's Fireworks" hung next to the door. She opened the door to the building and we entered.

There were lots of shelves. Aisles of shelves, loaded with various types of fireworks. One whole shelf was full of bottle rockets, another full of sparklers. A pudgy man in his fifties stood with a clipboard and a pen, counting the boxes. He looked at us when we approached.

"Hon, these folks are reporters from the *News*. They want to ask some questions about Glenn."

"Flip," said the man as he shook our hands. "What would you like to know?"

Kirk said, "Did you hear that James Alsbrook's son was killed in the bombing last week? I'm looking into his mining business and investigating some of the accidents he's linked to."

"I did hear that. He got what he deserved."

"That's a pretty strong statement," I said. "What do you know about the accident that killed your son?"

Mr. Coyne's eyes stayed on the clipboard. "I know that son of a bitch was told to fix the roof. He didn't. Fixin' it would have meant shutting the mine down for a few days. Glenn was killed by a falling rock. Huh, not a rock really, more like a boulder. It wouldn't have happened if Alsbrook had done what he was told to do."

Mrs. Coyne added, "He didn't die immediately. He had a closed head injury. We had to…" Her eyes were full of tears again. "We had to…unplug the life support." She was sobbing now. "He was twenty-five years old. He'd just met the nicest girl, too. Now I won't ever have grandchildren."

"He was your only child?" I asked.

"My only one."

I walked around and put my arm around Julia's shoulders. She sank into mine as she sobbed. Her husband looked uncomfortable.

"What was he like, Glenn?" Kirk asked.

Flip answered, "He was a clever kid. Liked to put things

together, you know? Did real good in school. I wanted him to come into the family business with me, but he said he wanted to do something for hisself first. He was going to join me later. The mine paid real good, see, and he was savin' for a truck. He wanted a new Ford, and a boat to go fishin' in."

Kirk pulled out a small notebook and wrote some things down, then asked, "Do you know what happened with the mine after the accident? Were there any consequences for what happened?"

"The mine safety folks came out and inspected again. Noted the ceiling hadn't been supported. They fined Alsbrook again and he paid it. Don't know if it's ever been fixed."

"Did you receive any compensation from the Alsbrooks?"

"Like money? Naw. Nothin'. He didn't even offer. I was gonna sue him. I wanted to sue him and make him pay, but then I found out how much money a lawyer is. And the lawyer said he probably had teams of attorneys we'd have to go up against. I couldn't afford it, you know? We have two busy seasons a year, and we have to make our money around New Year's Eve and the Fourth of July. I ain't rich."

Julia said, "There was one sweet lady, Dana something, who came out and offered to help with the burial costs, but we managed without her. Her son died in a mine accident, too."

"I am so sorry for what happened," I said. Julia and Flip nodded, like they'd heard that a lot. They agreed to let Kirk write about their son, and gave us a handsome picture of him. It was a photo of a young blond guy standing in front of an aluminum boat at a boat show. He seemed excited, pointing at a boat that sported two camouflage chairs for fishing.

"He loved to fish," Julia said. "He would go up to Smith Lake nearly every weekend and dreamed of owning a boat like that."

I could picture him on the boat as she said that. A quiet morning on a still lake, the only sound a small splash as he cast his line. I was sad for the dream that had died.

Kirk and I said our goodbyes and headed back to Birmingham. I was quiet on the way back.

Kirk asked, "What are you thinking about?"

"Oh, those poor parents. Losing their only son and having nothing for it. I wish they could have sued. I'm also thinking about the fact that Flip owns a firework business and may know about explosives."

"Fireworks with heavy explosives have been illegal since 1966. Things like cherry bombs and M-80s. So, he wouldn't really have access to the explosives."

"How do you know that?"

"I did a story on fireworks a few years ago."

"Doesn't mean he doesn't have the knowledge though."

"No, but fireworks and bombs are two different things. I don't think he's the guy."

"Because you really don't think so, or you don't want him to be?"

He smiled. "Maybe a little of both."

"When is this story going to run?"

"I hope within a week. I'm going to do a couple more interviews. I'd love your help. You have a way of comforting people that really helps."

"Well, I mean, they are grieving and it's tough for them."

"I lose sight of that sometimes. I have an appointment with the Kramer family on Saturday. They live up in Cullman. Will you go with me?"

"I have a family, you know."

"I know. We can go in the evening."

"I need to be home in the evenings. I have a kid now."

"You aren't going to go?"

"I'm sorry, Kirk. I just have a lot of responsibilities right now. I can't drop everything and run out to investigate with you. I'm sure you can handle it."

He was quiet after that until he dropped me back at work. "I'll call you after I talk to the Kramers."

"Thanks. Talk to you then."

I closed cases for a couple of hours and then picked Reese up at school. She handed me a grubby piece of paper with seven digits scrawled on it. "Thas' Sharonda's mom's number."

"Terrific. What's her name?"

LaReesa shrugged. "Shar's last name is Fowler."

"Okay, I'll give her a call."

I got Reese a snack and got her settled with her homework. She had missed a lot of it this week. Her teachers were being really understanding and letting her make it up. I was grateful to them for helping her adjust to her new school. I went into the living room and dialed the phone number on the piece of paper she'd given me. A woman answered.

"Is this Mrs. Fowler?"

"It is."

"This is Claire Conover, and I'm LaReesa Jones's foster

mom."

"Oh, right. Sharonda said you'd be calling."

"I'm sorry, I don't know your first name."

She laughed. "It's Cheryl. We'd love to have LaReesa over Saturday night."

"That's very kind. She and Sharonda seem to have formed a bond, and I'm trying to encourage her to make some friends her own age." I was sure Reese was eavesdropping, so I went back to my bedroom and closed the door behind me. "She has a history of hanging out with much older people, boys mostly. Men."

"Well, Chuck and I are going to take the girls to the Summit mall on Saturday, and we'll get them dinner there and then maybe stream some movies. We will keep a close eye on her, I promise."

"Please feel free to call me if she gives you any trouble at all. I can come pick her up at any time."

"I'm sure it will be fine. Sharonda's a good girl and, so far, hasn't made any bad decisions as far as friends go. She told us about Reese and a bit about her history. It's tough in a new school, especially when nobody looks like you. Sharonda's had a bit of trouble with that, too."

"I'm so glad she's found a friend her age, and race. This has been a bit a struggle for me, with the cultural differences and everything. She's my first foster child." I don't know why, but I felt I could talk to Cheryl about this.

"But don't you work at DHS?"

"I do, but I don't usually bring the kids home with me, at least not physically."

She laughed. "Sharonda's my third, so I've seen it all. My oldest daughter is twenty and a sophomore at Alabama State University, down in Montgomery. The next is my son, he's eighteen and in the Navy. Lord, we went through it with him. He wanted to be a rapper and join a gang when he was in junior high school. Walked around with his pants pulled halfway down and wearing red and talking about the Bloods. I was terrified he would be killed. Shar was my surprise baby five years after my son. So far, she has shown good sense. Very level headed and serious about her grades."

"I really appreciate this invitation. What time should I bring her over?"

"How about five o'clock? I hope you'll stay and have a glass of wine and chat."

"Sold. See you then." She gave me her address, which was in an area of nice houses that had recently been built on Dad's street. I liked Cheryl already, and hoped LaReesa wouldn't mess this up.

At nine-thirty the next morning we left for Sophistication, the hair place in Powderly. Reese was so excited; she'd been up since eight and was practically bouncing in the passenger seat next to me. And talking non-stop.

"I might get colored braids. Orange, maybe. Or pink. Or white. What do you think?"

The lady on the phone had told me the braids were going to be about a hundred dollars. "Are the colored ones more expensive?" I asked.

"I dunno. I can ask. Maybe I'll just get a couple, in the front."

It was good to see her so excited. I pulled up to a small building and parked in the driveway. It looked like someone's house.

The large front room had grubby, old linoleum on the floor and held six old, worn, beauticians' chairs. Three black women were working on customers, and talking loudly and laughing. Gospel music played on a radio from somewhere. One of the women spotted Reese and exclaimed, "Baby!" She was in her thirties and was dressed in an apron and in a pretty, short wig. She threw her arms around Reese in a big hug. Reese said, "Hey Ms. Vanessa!" and returned the hug. She turned to me and said, "Ms. Vanessa a friend of my mamma's." I nodded at that statement and looked for a place to sit down.

Vanessa shook my hand. "Thank you for taking care of this baby. You know, this is going to take several hours."

I hadn't thought about that. Vanessa continued, "Why don't you go have a day to yourself? We will take good care of her, I promise. She'll be ready about four."

"Oh, okay. And I'll pay you when I pick her up?"

"That will be fine."

I left the shop and considered what to do next. Grant was already running errands. I thought about calling him and decided against it. The weather was a little cool but beautiful. The temperature was in the mid-fifties and the sky a clear blue. I knew where I was heading.

Chapter Fourteen

I went home and changed into warm fleece-lined tights and an old long-sleeved flannel shirt with a t-shirt underneath. Then I put on my hiking boots with thick socks. I packed a small backpack with a sandwich and a bottle of water, grabbed a walking stick, and drove south.

Cahaba River Park was a large wilderness area in Shelby County, about twenty minutes south of where I lived. I could feel the stress easing as I pulled onto River Road. I parked the car at the Pavilion and pulled up the trail map on my phone.

I studied the map for a minute and decided to do the trail called Rust Bucket, the one that followed the cliffs above the Cahaba River for a bit. With the leaves off the trees, I would even get a view of the river during my hike. I strapped on my backpack, grabbed my stick, and headed for the trail head.

The first part of the hike was through the dense woods, mostly pine trees. The path itself was about two feet wide, packed dirt covered in dead pine needles and brown oak leaves, which softened the sound of my boots. I put one boot in front of the other, planting my walking staff with each step. I loved the woods section of this trail because it was so remarkably *quiet*. Occasionally, I heard the caw of a bird, but beyond that there were no sounds other than the ones I was making. No traffic. No planes. I was in heaven.

Grant liked to hike, too, and now and then on the weekends we would visit local parks. There was one very close to my neighborhood called Moss Rock Preserve that featured very short, steep trails. It was a good place to hike for an hour or so just to get outdoors. There was Oak Mountain as well, where several months ago I had been followed while investigating little Michael Hennessy's death. I still shuddered at that memory.

I dreamed of one day taking a month to hike part of the Appalachian Trail. I had some friends who had done that for a couple of weeks and said it was unreal. They talked at length about people who lived on the trail permanently, about the shelters set up for stormy weather and how they had to share the space with strangers during a storm. Hikers could camp along the trail as well, which I would love to do. I always thought a hike like that would make a good honeymoon, if I ever got married.

Grant and I had never talked about getting married, at least not yet. I hiked up some switchbacks to a ridge in the woods while I thought about that. We were comfortable living together, and I loved him, and he said he loved me, so maybe marriage was in the future. *As long as he didn't find out about Kirk.* We'd been a couple since July, and roommates for a month. We were still early in this whole thing. It was really too early to talk about marriage, right?

I fantasized about a wedding for a while. I always wanted an outdoor wedding, in my hometown, in the late spring at Aldridge Gardens among the hydrangeas. The man who had founded Aldridge Gardens had discovered and patented the Snowflake Hydrangea, and the park was full of them. The park was beautiful, with a large lake and lots of native Alabama plants and flowers. I'd have a simple white dress, my Dad in a tuxedo, with just a couple of attendants. Royanne as my bridesmaid, and Grant would have a groomsman, too…

Of course, nothing about my behavior recently showed that I was ready to get married, or apparently be faithful. The guilt ate at my gut again and I could feel it in my stomach. I wanted to tell Grant what happened. Come clean and beg his forgiveness. But what if I didn't get it? He'd move out and never speak to me again. I deserved that, I realized. No, I'd keep what happened with Kirk a secret. Forever. I didn't want one evening of weakness to ruin this.

I hiked up another ridge and reached the spot where the Cahaba River was visible over the high, steep cliff. I picked a fallen tree to sit on and opened my backpack to retrieve the sandwich and the bottle of water. The view was beautiful. The river was relatively still today, its color a sage green. I ate slowly, as my mind wandered back to Marcus Freedman and his baby granddaughter. And the bombing and Jason Alsbrook.

Other than race, I couldn't see why anyone would want Marcus dead. That was enough of a motive for some people, but if that was it, then I expected someone would come forward and claim responsibility. Of course, Marcus hadn't died, so maybe they didn't want to claim this failure. And I was really afraid they were going to try again. But if Jason was the intended victim, why? It just felt like it all pointed back to his father, James. There seemed to be no shortage of people who wished him ill. I thought about Flip Coyne's angry answers to Kirk's questions. How many others were there, who felt the same way?

I finished my lunch and carefully packed up all the trash. I followed the river for twenty yards or so, until the trail turned and headed back toward the road. I still had a long hike down the trail to the car. I walked, listening to the birds and the light breeze in the trees. I breathed deep. The air was cold but fresh, my breath showing a bit of condensation each time I exhaled. My mind went back to my wedding fantasy. I thought about flowers as I headed down toward the car at a slow pace.

My watch read nearly one o'clock, and I had three hours until I had to pick up LaReesa. The walk to the car took most of an hour. By the time I reached my Honda my mind was clear and I felt great. I drove back to Bluff Park, stopping at the ATM at the bank along the way. I got home and took a long shower, and by the time I finished Grant was home.

"Hey, where've you been?"

"I dropped Reese off to get her hair done, then went out to Cahaba River Park and hiked."

"Oh, that sounds fun. You should have called me."

"I thought you were busy."

"I could have come home."

"Sorry, I just needed to some time to myself."

"You need a lot of that lately."

His tone annoyed me. "I needed to clear my head. Some other time? We could go tomorrow?"

"Yeah, maybe."

"I've got to go pick up LaReesa. She's going to go spend the night with a friend tonight."

"Good luck to them."

"What's that supposed to mean?"

"You really trust her to behave? Not to get high? Not sneak out to be with some boy?"

"I have to start somewhere. You always seem to want to start with what she is going to do wrong."

"I think it's necessary to prepare for the worst."

"That's a pessimistic way to look at the world."

"I don't like surprises."

The guilt in my gut showed itself again and I looked away toward the floor. He walked back to the office and I went to Powderly to pick up Reese. I was there just before four and when I arrived, she was sitting in one of the beautician's chairs, laughing and joking with Vanessa and the other women. She stood up and walked toward me.

"What d'ya think?"

Her hair was done in narrow braids all over that hung past her shoulders, and at her temples were two braids that were black and orange. Someone had given her some orange-tinted lipstick and some sparkly eyeshadow and eyeliner, and she looked beautiful. I told her so.

"Thanks. Thanks for letting me do this." I paid Vanesssa the one hundred and ten dollars she asked for and we headed home.

"That was so much fun," she said in the car. "I've really missed Ms. Vanessa. She so nice. She been writin' to my mamma, and Mamma says she wants to get clean."

"What do you think about that?"

"She done said that before, when she had me with her. She din' do it though, so I don't believe her."

"Sometimes it takes a few tries, and it helps to be in treatment."

"She said she din' have no time to go to no damn meetins. Said they was stupid, anyways."

I'd heard the same thing from countless addicts after I'd taken their children away. "It helps if you are willing to try. You have to want to stop."

"She's stopped now, in jail."

"I hope she can stay clean. Listen, when we get home, you have to pack pretty quickly. We are due at the Fowler's at five. Ms. Fowler says you and Sharonda are going to the mall, and will have dinner there."

"Can I have some money? I mean, to pay for my dinner?"

I had anticipated this question and taken out some extra money so she could have a bit to shop. "Yes, and I got a bit extra in case you want to buy something. Be reasonable, though, and if it's too low cut, I'm going to take it away."

"You think everything is too low cut."

"Because it is, for a thirteen-year-old."

She sighed. "So ol' school."

LaReesa packed a tote bag I found for her when we got home. She changed into clean jeans and a cute sweater and played with her hair endlessly. I gave her forty dollars and finally loaded her in the car.

"Can I have my phone?"

"No, you lost the privilege of having a phone after inviting those men over and getting high. You'll get it back on Wednesday."

"Wednesday? Damn!"

"You want to stay home tonight?"

"No."

I turned into the driveway of the address Cheryl Fowler had given me. It was a large, new home further down on the same street my father lived on, with a similar, gorgeous view of Jones Valley. I parked the car and followed LaReesa to the stained-glass front door.

She rang the bell and it was opened by Sharonda, dressed in a cute-patterned dress with tights. They greeted each other and Sharonda invited us in.

Chapter Fifteen

The door opened into a foyer with a huge, beautiful staircase that curved up to the second story. The banister on the stairs was an intricate wood pattern that I loved, and it complemented the wood floors. A large, round window above the door filled the room with soft light. The walls were stucco and painted a pretty cream color.

"Whoa," I heard Reese mutter.

Sharonda said, "Your hair looks so cute. I love it." The two of them vanished up the stairs, already giggling.

Cheryl appeared from the back of the house. She was a pretty black woman, with short, natural hair and a cute smile. "Come on in."

"Thanks for doing this, for taking Reese out. Please call me immediately if she gives you any trouble."

"I'm sure she'll be fine." She led me back to a gorgeous kitchen, with all stainless appliances and gray and white quartz countertops. To the right hung large windows showing an amazing view of the valley. I sat in front of the enormous island and Cheryl brought out two bottles.

"Red or white?" she asked.

"White." She poured a glass for me and one for herself. The wine was a Pinot Grigio, which was light and tart and delicious. "This house is gorgeous."

"Thank you. Chuck and I had it built a few years ago. We love it here."

"What do you do?"

"I'm a Human Resources person for a bank. Chuck works for a different bank, and he's a financial planner."

"Which bank?"

"Mine is Birmingham Financial."

"Oh, that's Roy's bank! You know Royanne Fayard?"

"Sure, she's so sweet."

"We've been best friends since we were ten." The wine rolled over my tongue, cool and delicious. I felt myself relax.

"Are you married?"

"No, I live with my boyfriend, Grant."

"And LaReeesa's been with you for how long?"

I laughed. "About a week and a half. It's been an adventure."

"Oh, so she's really just getting settled."

"Yeah. It's been a little hard for her, the new school and everything. She is way behind in her studies."

"But a bright girl, right?"

"Very."

"She'll adjust. It takes time. What made you guys want to foster?"

"I work for DHS, in the Department of Child Services. I met Reese last year when I was investigating a whole different case. I should have opened a case on her and her cousins then, but I decided not to, then her grandmother died and she disappeared. She was on the street for about four months. She hasn't shared a whole lot of details about that, but I'm sure it wasn't easy."

"Poor baby. Is she going to stay with you permanently?"

"I hope so. The answer to that question is going to depend a lot on her behavior, and her mother's. I know living with me, here, is quite a culture shock, and I have no idea how to help her through that. I'm honestly so thrilled she's found a friend in Sharonda. Are you from here?" I asked.

"I grew up over in Bessemer, and went to Jess Lanier high school before it closed, so I understand the culture shock."

"That was a rough school," I said. Jess Lanier used to be the main high school for Bessemer, a town west of Birmingham. The population was mostly African-American, and the crime rate and gang violence in the past had been very high.

"Very rough. Lots of gangs and guns. We would have 'Code Purple' called at school, and that meant a gun on campus. This was around the time of Columbine and it was terrifying."

I thought back to my high school days. We never had a Code anything, and no one ever brought a gun there. We never had active-shooter drills. My biggest stressors in high school were my grades, boys, and increasing my ACT score. I was reminded once again to check my privilege. I said, "I was lucky. I grew up here, and we never had a school shooting, or even a gun on campus."

"I had a mamma who drilled it into me that the way out was education. I studied hard and got a scholarship to Tuskegee. Got a degree in Business Admin, which led me to human resources. How did you wind up in social work?"

"My dad, who lives literally down the road from you, is a therapist. I grew up in a house where taking care of others was important. When I got to college, social work just fit with everything I wanted to do and believed. I got a job in child welfare and never looked back."

"You love it?"

I laughed. "Most days I really do. So many of these kids are resilient. They've been to hell and back and somehow rebound. It's amazing. It's the ones who don't who haunt me."

"Like LaReesa?"

I shrugged and lowered my voice, in case Reese was listening. "I don't know how she is going to wind up, frankly. She's bright, but an education has never been stressed to her. As I was telling Grant the other day, she's never seen anyone get up and go to work before. Her mother worked the streets, and her grandmother stayed home raising her grandbabies. There's never been a man or a father in her life. I worry about it."

"Let me spend some time with her. I think it's important for young black girls to see successful black women."

"Very important. I'd appreciate that."

There was a clamor of noise on the stairs and the girls entered the kitchen. Both now had makeup on and Reese's hair was pulled back into a printed cloth headband. It looked cute.

"Mom, can we go? Where's Dad?"

"Dad is going to meet us there."

I swallowed the last bit of the wine, stood up and took LaReesa's hands. "Promise me you are going to make good decisions. Mrs. Fowler is going to call me if you give her even a little bit of trouble. I will come get you in a hot second."

"I promise. Damn."

"Language."

"Sorry."

I thanked Cheryl again for everything and said goodbye to the girls. The ride home took ten minutes, and Grant was home when I got in.

He kissed me and asked if I had thought about dinner. "I haven't, what do you think?"

"Wanna go try that pizza place down the hill?"

"Let me change."

"Me, too."

I swapped my jeans and sweatshirt for a tunic and tights and boots, grabbed my jacket and met Grant in the van. He had put on dark jeans and a cute plaid button-down. His brown hair was curly and sexy and I told him so. I got a smile for that.

He drove to South Shades Crest road and headed for Oxmoor Road. He was quiet on the drive, and I spent much of the short journey glued to my phone, waiting for some word from Cheryl. That didn't change once we entered Pizzeria GM. Bright posters and signs covered the walls. The place was crowded and loud with patrons and music, and we had to sit at the "pizza bar"; a long, wooden bench overlooking the kitchen and the large pizza oven. We could feel the heat from the oven in our seats. The view of the open kitchen was kind of cool and we sat and watched the staff as they put pies together.

A waitress brought us menus and we scanned them. I had my phone in hand and kept checking it as Grant commented on the menu. "All these pizzas look amazing. I might get the one with pimento cheese and jalapenos."

"Hmm." I responded. I had installed Life360 on Reese's phone, which was an app I could use to check her location. Of course, I couldn't do that when she didn't have it on her. That was one downside to taking it away. I thought about calling Cheryl to check on things, and began to scroll through my recent calls when Grant suddenly snatched my phone out of my hands.

"Hey!" I cried.

"Dammit, I'm trying here. I'm trying to talk to you and enjoy our night out. Why does everything always have to be about LaReesa?"

"She's spending the night away for the first time. I'm worried about her."

"That girl spent four months on the street. She is perfectly capable of taking care of herself. Let it go."

"I'm afraid she's going to get in trouble."

"Then we'll deal with that when it happens. I'll keep an eye on your phone."

Now it felt like *I* was the one being punished, and I was mad. "Give me the goddamn phone, Grant."

"No. You need to relax and eat something. What do you want?"

"My phone."

"No. Pick something."

I wasn't hungry. I wasn't going to pick something just because he ordered me to do so. "I want to go home."

"No, I'm hungry and you are acting like a petulant child."

"I'm acting like a concerned parent, which is what I hoped you'd be."

"I never got a vote about being one in the first place."

The song changed on the speakers overhead and seemed to get louder. *Blinding Lights* by The Weekend blasted through them, the beat thumping against the loud chatter of the other diners. The kitchen staff called out orders to each other and a chair scraped across the floor. I stood up.

"I'm going to get some air." I grabbed my jacket and headed for the door. He didn't follow me.

I walked to the small parking lot by the side of the building and began to pace. I was tense, and angry, and that wasn't helping the situation. I tried to see things from Grant's perspective. He was right, he didn't really get a vote in where Reese would live. I brought her home in the middle of the night like a stray dog and didn't let him have a say in it. I knew I should ask him if he wanted her to stay. I was afraid of the answer.

My affair with Kirk wasn't helping things, either. A vision of his naked, lean, muscular body entered my conscious, unbidden. I shook my head to clear it and paced faster. Grant exited the restaurant and joined me. "You're still here."

"You have the keys. And my phone."

"Come inside and let's eat."

I followed him, mostly because I had no other choice. We returned to our seats and I shrugged when Grant asked me what I wanted. He ordered the pizza he had mentioned earlier, and I ordered a glass of Sauvignon Blanc, which brought back more images of naked Kirk. I drank the wine and ordered another, drank that quickly and got a little buzzed. Grant and I didn't speak.

The pizza arrived, and looked delicious with pimento cheese, smoked sausage and jalapenos. I picked the peppers off and choked down a slice. It tasted like sawdust. We finished our meal in silence and Grant paid the check and we went home.

"I'm going to bed," he announced.

"I'm going to stay up and read for a while. Can I have my phone?"

He handed it to me and I immediately unlocked it and checked for calls.

"Goodnight," Grant said.

"Yeah, night," I responded, pulling up my texts. He left the room.

The guilt kicked in again as I thought about calling Cheryl. I checked my clock, it was eight-thirty. I texted the number for her that Reese had given me.

Everything ok?

No response.

Chapter Sixteen

I checked the screen again. Why wouldn't Cheryl text me back? Was Reese in trouble? Finally, my phone rang.

Not Cheryl. Kirk. "Hey beautiful, what's up? You busy tonight?"

"No."

"You okay?"

"Yes." I wasn't about to share my relationship problems with him.

"I went and saw the Kramers today. Nice couple. Elderly, very. Mr. Kramer could hardly get out of his chair and Mrs. Kramer is on a walker. Timothy was their youngest child of six, and had worked in the Gate Mine for only a week when he was killed in a fire. Once again, James was warned that it could happen and did nothing. I don't see how he lives with himself."

"Mm."

"Anyway, I need to go see Ronnie Parks's family tomorrow. Will you go with me? Please? His mom is a single parent and lives in the Wylam neighborhood. I could really use some help."

Getting out of the house and away from Grant sounded like a great idea. "LaReesa's out tonight, spending the night with a friend. I have to pick her up in the morning, but then I'm free."

"I'll pick you up at one?"

"Does this woman know we are coming?"

"I called her today and said I would firm something up in the morning. Her name is Gayle Parks."

"Okay, see you at one."

Ten minutes later I finally got a text from Cheryl. *Home from mall. Everything fine. Can you pick Reese up at noon tomorrow? We are going to take the girls out for breakfast.*

Absolutely. Thanks so much, again. I texted back.

Hope you and Grant had a wonderful evening. See you tomorrow.

Not so much, I thought. I slept on the couch.

The next day, I pulled into the Fowler's driveway at exactly noon, and Reese walked out burdened with her tote bag and two large plastic bags from the mall. I got out of the car and went to help her.

"Good Lord." I said, loading the bags into the trunk.

"The Fowler's bought my dinner at the Cheesecake Factory."

I shot her a look.

"They did. They insisted. So I spent all th' money you gave me on clothes and stuff. It's all cute, and none of it is low-cut."

I laughed. "Good. I want to see it when we get home. You had a good time, then?"

"I had a great time. Ms. Cheryl was talkin' to me about what I wanna do when I get older."

"What did you say?"

"I wanna do hair. She said I have to go to cosmo…cosmo something school to get a license."

"Cosmetology school."

"Yeah, that's it. Ms. Vanessa went to one in Midfield and said I'd do well if I stick to it."

"You talked to Vanessa about this?"

"Yeah, when I saw her yesterday. She say I got to graduate high school to get in, though."

Thank God for Ms. Vanessa, I thought. "What do you think about that?"

"I think I gotta study."

"I think you're right."

I pulled into the carport at my house and noted Grant's van was gone. I helped Reese unload all of the stuff to her room. She showed me three shirts she bought, along with a pair of printed tights and some fun socks. She had a lot of clothes in the bags, though, and explained that Sharonda had a bunch of stuff she didn't want any more so she had given it to Reese. All of the clothes were cute, and appropriate, and I told Reese I was proud of her for her choices.

Grant got home as we were putting it all away and popped his head in for an update. Reese offered us a fashion show and we sat on opposite sides of the couch in the living room as she changed.

"Where were you earlier?" I asked.

"I had to run to the office for a minute. I'm installing a security system."

"Listen," I said, "I've got to go out for a while at one. Can you please keep an eye on Reese for me?"

"Where are you going?"

"Kirk Mahoney and I have to go do an interview."

"Kirk Mahoney? The reporter? I though you weren't going to hang around with him anymore."

"I know, but he's researching some stuff having to do with one of my cases, and he needs my help." *And I want to get out of here*, I thought.

"I seriously doubt that. He managed to do his job just fine before he met you."

I ignored that. "So will you watch her?"

"Of course. Someone has to." I let that go, too. "Thanks."

We saw Reese's new shirts and tights and told her how beautiful she looked. All of the clothes she bought still had the tags on, and I had some doubts about the other stuff. It looked too new to be a discard from Sharonda. I thought about the money that had gone missing from Grant's shop and wondered if LaReesa had stolen the clothes, or bought them with stolen money. I'd have to ask Cheryl about it later.

Kirk pulled into the driveway at one but didn't come to the door. I said goodbye to Reese and Grant, and got no response from Grant. Reese said "Bye," and turned on the TV.

Kirk headed for the interstate once I was strapped in his silver Infiniti.

"Where are we heading?"

"Wylam."

"You told me that. Where?"

"A neighborhood called Wylam Oaks?"

I knew it. I'd been on investigations close by there. Wylam Oaks was a neighborhood built several years ago by Habitat for Humanity. The land had been donated by U.S. Steel and the houses were new and cute, sat in the shadow of the U.S. Steel plant.

Several minutes later Kirk pulled into Nebraska Circle and scanned the mailboxes for a number. He parked in front of a small, white house with bright red shutters. "This is it," he said, undoing his seat belt.

"What's her name again?"

"Gayle Parks. Are you okay? You seem really distracted."

"Yeah, I've got a lot going on."

"Did you tell Grant about our night together?"

"No! I told you, I don't want to discuss it. It never happened."

"Too bad, because it was fantastic."

I shot him a look. "Please stop saying things like that."

"Why? I like you, and I'd like a chance to have something more than friendship."

"No. I love Grant, and I'm going to try to make this work." I got out of the car. Kirk followed me to the front door and knocked.

It was opened by a black woman in her early forties, still dressed in a brown uniform for a chain breakfast restaurant. Her nametag said Gayle and her curly hair was pulled back with a headband. She looked exhausted. "Ms. Parks? I'm Kirk Mahoney, we spoke on the phone earlier?"

"Of course. Please come in. I just got off work, so please excuse the way I look." She led us into an attractive living room filled with oversized, red furniture and a large glass coffee table. She invited us to have a seat and we sunk into the sofa.

"You look fine," I said. "What time did you have to be at work this morning?"

"Four," she said. "I'm hoping to grab some sleep before I go to my second job at Wal-Mart at three. I'll get off there at eleven tonight."

So many women and men led a life like hers, I thought. Working constantly, and one illness or missed paycheck from homelessness and disaster.

Kirk said, "I'm doing a story on the mining accidents in our state recently. Your son was killed in the Warm Creek Mine disaster, correct? Do you mind talking to us about your son?" he asked.

Gayle nodded. "Sure, but I dunno what good it's gonna do. Can't nothing bring him back."

"How old was he when he was killed?"

"Ronnie was twenty. He'd worked in the mine for four months. A friend of mine, Dana, said the mine had been warned that this accident might happen. They didn't do nothing to fix it. Her son was killed that day, too."

"We've met with Dana and heard about B.B. That's a large part of why I'm writing this story, to try to get some justice for the victims. What was Ronnie like?"

Gayle smiled. "He was a good kid. Managed to avoid all the bad stuff around here, you know? Never joined a gang or got busted for anything. No problems with drugs or alcohol or some of the other stuff I've seen with my friends' kids. He had a real interest in music, but I just couldn't afford to send him to college. He started working at a fast food place in high school and was a real hard worker. He was on his way to becoming a manager, before he quit that job to go work in the mine. I wish I could've done more for him."

Kirk was writing in his notebook. I asked, "What about his father? Was he close to him?" I looked around the room for signs that anyone else lived here, but didn't see any.

"Ronnie's dad and I never married. I was sixteen when I got pregnant, and he was eighteen. We were only together for a couple of months, but he was always real good about providing for him. Sent child support checks until the very day Ronnie turned eighteen."

"Where's his dad now?" Kirk asked.

"Oh, he still lives around here somewhere. He went in the army right after Ronnie was born, but he's back now. I heard he got a job working for some rich-ass dude in Mountain Brook. His job provides him with an apartment and everything."

I felt the room go very, very cold and the little blond hairs on my arm stood up. Kirk and I looked at each other and I asked, "What's Ronnie's dad's name?"

"Ronald. Ronald Cushman."

Chapter Seventeen

I took a deep breath to steady my nerves. "Did you know Ronald works for the same guy who owns the mine your son was killed in?" I asked.

"Really?" Cheryl said. She was silent for a few seconds as that sunk in. "He never told me the rich guy's name."

"How long has he worked for him; do you know?" Kirk asked.

"About three years," she answered. "Damn, I was so happy for him, too."

Kirk took a few pictures of Gayle, then she gave us one of Ronnie taken before he died. A young, fit black man in a suit with a high school diploma in his hands that read "Johnson High School." Gayle had tears in her eyes.

"He was so proud when he graduated. He had friends who didn't, see. One was killed in a drive-by, three dropped out. He wanted to work and be successful."

"He seems like a wonderful young man," I agreed. I was anxious to leave, and Kirk's foot was bouncing up and down as he sat next to me. He asked a few more questions. Gayle, like Dana, had not been given anything after Ronnie's death. No compensation from the Alsbrooks, nor any help with the funeral costs. It had eaten all of her savings to lay him to rest. Dana had stepped in and helped, which spurred the idea for the Mourned Miners.

"Dana has done so much," Gayle said through tears. "She meets with everybody after an accident. I don't see how she does it."

I said, softly, "She does it for B.B. To keep his spirit alive."

I was ready for Kirk to wind up so we could get on the road. He thanked Gayle for her time and said the article would be out soon. We practically ran for his Infiniti after we left.

We strapped ourselves in and he raced, I mean raced, to the Interstate. I held on tight to the handle on the door and tried to breathe. "Wow."

"I'm headed for James's house."

"Yeah, I think Ronald has a few questions to answer. I mean, this could be a total coincidence. Maybe he doesn't realize who he works for,"

Kirk scoffed. "Nope. Not buying that."

"Yeah, me neither."

He whipped around the curve at Malfunction Junction and I gripped the door handle tighter. "But I don't get it. He's been there for three years, since just after his son died. I mean, if he's planning something…"

"Maybe it took him three years to pull it off." Kirk checked his GPS and decided to stay on I-65. We sped to the Lakeshore Boulevard exit and I checked to make sure the door was locked so I wouldn't fly out. He weaved in an out of the traffic as I clenched my teeth and thought.

"I don't get it. He had really nice things to say about James."

"I don't either. He has a few things to explain." He raced to Mountain Brook and my heart beat at top speed as he took the curves. We reached James's house and he stopped at the guard gate. The guard house next to it was empty. The gate was open and we noted a frenzy of activity near the wide-open front door.

One sedan and three police cars were parked in the drive, in front of the house. Two of them had their lights flashing. A uniformed officer was entering one of the cars and greeted us with a nod. He drove away down the hill as Kirk and I entered the house. We made our way to the dark green living room with the fireplace where we had been before. The fireplace was bare today. Two uniformed officers stood on each side of the door. James was there, barefoot, and dressed in khakis and an untucked striped button-down, shouting at a man in a wrinkled suit.

"I want you to find my wife! She's been kidnapped, you idiot!"

"But sir, she hasn't. It says here she left of her own accord. She's an adult, and is allowed to leave." He held a piece of notebook paper with half of the page covered in tiny handwriting.

"She was probably forced to write that at gunpoint. She is in danger and you aren't doing anything! If she dies…"

"I'm sorry. As I've explained, this clearly states her intention to leave." He handed the paper to James, and said, "We will not file a missing person report on her, nor will we do a BOLO."

James noticed us for the first time and said, "Oh fuck. What the hell do you want?"

"To speak to you," Kirk said.

"No! Get out! I have no comment."

I interceded. "Mr. Alsbrook, if Patricia has left, Mr. Mahoney can help get the word out and help you find her."

The man in the suit, who I assumed was a detective, nodded at us. "I'll be going." He handed the piece of paper to James and left.

James was turning red. His face looked older somehow, the gray stubble on his chin and the creases in his skin became more visible the redder he got. He handed the sheet of paper to Kirk.

"Ronald, that son of a bitch, has kidnapped my wife. I can't believe he did this. I trusted him!"

Kirk held the piece of paper so we could both read it. Patricia's handwriting was so small and neat, I almost had to squint.

James,

Ronald and I have left. Please do not make any attempt to find us. Ronald has been so helpful the past couple of years, helping me to deal with your behavior and Jason's death. He loves me, and I love him. We are going far away from here where we can live together in love and happiness. I won't come back. I should have left you years ago, when the abuse started. I'm so sorry that Jason had to grow up with a father like you. I wish I could say that to him.

His death is your fault. You have let so many people die because you did not repair the problems in your mines. Not to mention all your abuse of me. I know God will provide His judgment, and you will get what you deserve.

Patricia

"Wow," I muttered. Go Patricia, I thought. I hoped she was well and far away from here by now.

"When did she leave?" Kirk asked.

"She was gone this morning when I woke up. She said she didn't feel well last night and was going to sleep in the downstairs guest room. It doesn't look like she's been in there at all. She's left all her clothes, and her cell phone."

So you can't track her, I thought. Go girl.

Kirk asked, "Did Ronald live here? Or nearby?"

"He lived in the apartment over the garage. For free, I might add, as part of his contract with me."

"Can we see the apartment?"

"I went out there first thing. It's empty, except for the furniture that was there when he moved in."

"Can we see it anyway?"

We followed him out of the front door and to the three-car garage behind the house. A metal staircase on the side of the building led to a small landing and a wooden door. James opened it wide. "See? Gone."

We entered a large studio apartment with two large windows that overlooked the woods behind the garage. To the left I saw an open kitchen, complete with electric stove and a full-sized fridge, and an island. At the far side of the room, a queen-sized bed neatly made with a blue-printed comforter stood in front of one of the windows. A small wooden dresser was against the far wall. Next to the dresser was the door to the bathroom, and next to that was a closet. The only other furniture in the room was a large, dark green sofa with a small television on a stand in front of it.

Kirk headed for the closet. The door was ajar, and a look inside revealed nothing but empty hangers. Nothing sat on the floor or the shelf. The bathroom was also empty of all personal possessions. A search of the couch yielded thirty-five cents in change. All of the kitchen supplies were still in the cabinets, but nothing else.

"What do you know about Ronald?" Kirk asked. "Anything about his personal life?"

"He grew up in Birmingham. I think he has a son. I don't know how old he is."

Kirk and I shared a glance. James apparently didn't know that Ronald's son was dead, or that he had died in one of James's mines. Kirk didn't seem to want to disclose that information at the moment, so I followed his lead and kept quiet.

"Ever mention any friends, other family members?"

"No. He was my employee. We didn't discuss personal matters. I have to go. I have to get on the phone with a private investigator and start the search for Patricia."

"But she doesn't want to be found," I said.

James turned to me in a sudden, full rage. His whole body seemed to grow larger as he moved toward me and he brought his hand back like he was about to slap me. I stepped back, quickly. "I don't give a fuck what she wants! It is not up to her! Get off my property, both of you, or I'll call the police back here and have you arrested."

He followed us out to Kirk's car and watched as we drove away.

"Damn, I hope she is hell and gone," I said.

"Me, too."

"Where are we headed?"

"I'm going to drop you off at home and go work on trying to locate Ronald. I also have a story to write. Two stories to write now."

"You going to include this?"

"Of course. James didn't say I couldn't."

I laughed. "Remember those lawyers your editor mentioned?"

He laughed, too. "Yeah, I gotta call them as well."

"I feel like I should do something. Try to find her. Where will you start?"

"I'm going to start by looking into Ronald's background. Friends from high school, and the army. Family. That sort of thing. But first I have to write this story."

"I want to go with you. I want to do something."

"I love hanging out with you, too."

"That's not what I meant."

"That's disappointing. I really hoped we could see more of each other."

I've already seen all of you, I thought. The guilt weighed on me again. "Look, I'm sorry about what happened. I should have been more careful. I was having a bad day, and you helped me feel better, at least temporarily. But I really want to try to work on things with Grant."

"I take it things aren't going well?"

"I don't know. I kinda sprung this foster kid on him literally overnight. He's adjusting, but I don't think he wants to be a parent right now."

"So she has to go?"

"Not right now, I don't think. I mean, I could put her in another foster home, but I don't think she'd stay there. She and I have formed a bond of sorts. I really like her. She's feisty. We are just taking it day by day."

Kirk turned the Infinity onto my street. "Good luck. I'll call you when I know something."

I got out of the car at the foot of my drive. Grant's van was in the street, and my car was in the single-car carport. I considered getting in the car and going…somewhere. I wondered if I could disappear like Patricia and Ronald. I stood in the driveway and thought about that for a minute. I had no idea where I'd go. All my friends lived here. I could go to my brother's house in Florida, maybe. But then who would check on my dad? Not to mention money. I'd have to earn some, somehow. I had a house and a kid, now, too. The adult thing to do would be to go inside and check on things.

Chapter Eighteen

I walked in through the carport and put my purse down in its place. Grant and Reese were at the dining room table, working on math homework. Grant was looking tense, his jaw clenched and a little furrow had formed between his eyebrows. "Hi," he said.

"Hi." I kissed him on the cheek.

"We are working on proportional relationships," he said.

Reese put her head face down on her arms on the table, her voice muffled as she added, "I don't know why I gotta know this. I wanna do hair."

"Math is important. You are going to have to work with chemicals to do hair, right?" Grant said.

"Yeah."

"Well, that's math and chemistry. Formulas and stuff. You wouldn't want to mess up somebody's hair, right? Put the wrong amount of something on and all the hair falls out?"

LaReesa giggled at that. I added, "Can you imagine? All the ladies in Midfield walking around bald?"

LaReesa and Grant were laughing hard now. Grant said, "You might start a new trend, baldness in women. People would line up around the block for LaReesa's new anti-hair treatments."

I went back to the bedroom to change, leaving them chuckling over math. I was glad to see it was going well. I put on comfy clothes and took my phone to the living room. I could hear Grant explaining the numbers in his calming voice.

He joined me after a while. "Math is done. She is working on Social Studies now. She's getting a little more patient with the math."

"I'm glad. Thanks so much for helping her."

"She really is a cool kid."

"I think so. And you are okay with her staying here? I know we didn't really talk about it when it happened, and I'm sorry. It was the middle of the night when I got the call."

"I know."

"And?"

"This is your house. You say who lives here, or not.'

"It's your house, too."

"Is it? I'm not so sure."

"Of course, it is."

Grant changed the subject. "I'm putting together a casserole for supper."

"That sounds good. I've got to go get some work done."

I went back to the office and booted up my laptop. I had a case to review and a court report to write, both of which got done fairly quickly. On a whim, I Googled "Ronald Cushman".

A number of things came up. A few FaceBook pages for several men with that name. I bookmarked them for later. I went back to Google and scrolled down. There were some obituaries, one from Illinois and one from Washington. A couple of LinkedIn profiles. I went back to FaceBook. The first four Ronalds were a bust. They were from areas of the country far away from here. But then...

There was no profile picture, or cover photo. And only two posts. One was from September 17, four years ago. There was a picture of a younger Ronald Senior, holding a toddler that seemed to be about two. He appeared to be tickling the boy as they both laughed. The kid was dressed in cute denim overalls with a red shirt. Both he and his dad had big smiles on their faces. The caption read: "Rest in peace my sweet boy. See you on the other side." There was a link to his obituary. The only other post was from three years ago, on the same date. "Hard to believe it's been a year already. I miss you every day."

I clicked on the link to the obituary.

Ronald Darrius "Ronnie" Parks

Ronald Darrius "Ronnie" Parks died September 16 at the Warm Creek #3 mine. Services will be held September 22 at Remembrance Funeral Home, Wylam. Burial will follow at Oak Gardens Cemetery. Visitation is from 6 to 8pm Thursday at the funeral home. Remembrance Funeral Home is directing.

He is preceded in death by his grandparents, Bernard and Penelope Cushman, and Elmer and Rose Parks. Survivors include his mother, Gayle Parks, and his father Ronald D. Cushman, both of Birmingham.

Honorary pallbearers are the Local UMWA 2257.

Benjamin Burke's obituary was there as well. Worded much the same, with the survivors his parents, Dana and Benjamin Burke. Before their marriage fell apart, I noted. Such a sad event. I wrote down the names of Ronnie's family, thinking I would pass them along to Kirk.

Sometime later my phone chimed. It was a text from Kirk. *My editor is going to run story about Priscilla tomorrow, with the*

James story on Sunday. Lead story! A smile emoji followed. I could hardly begin to imagine what James's reaction to that was going to be. His crimes and family drama for all the world to see. I was bummed I had to wait a week, and texted that to Kirk.

The next day was Martin Luther King, Jr. Day and I had the day off. The entrance fee to the Birmingham Civil Rights Museum was waived. I proposed a trip to LaReesa, although the museum was likely to be crowded. She said she didn't want to wait in line forever to see the museum, and would rather stay home and order pizza and watch movies. So we did.

Tuesday, Maddie Freedman had a well-baby check with the pediatrician that Marcus and Betty Ann had chosen, and I went to pick them up just before lunch for the appointment. When I got to Marcus's house, several cars were in the street, including one police car. I hurried from my Honda to the front door and knocked.

Deborah Holt, the FBI agent, answered the door and greeted me as I stepped inside. "What's going on?" I asked.

Agent Holt looked at Betty Ann, who stood near the kitchen door. She'd been crying, and I could see the tear stains on her cheeks. She held little Maddie, who was making random noises as she twisted her grandmother's beaded necklace. Marcus sat on the couch, talking to two men in suits as a uniformed police officer wrote something down.

Betty Ann answered me. "We've gotten a letter. You just missed the bomb squad." Her eyes filled with tears again.

Marcus added, "They didn't find anything. They did a thorough search with dogs, even under the house. I have to watch out for packages mailed here, and I've hired a security firm. What are you doing here?"

"Maddie has a doctor's appointment in an hour."

"Oh, hell. I totally forgot," said Betty Ann.

"Do you want me to reschedule?" I pulled out my phone.

"No, no. We need to get out of here, anyway."

We both looked to the front window as two cars pulled up. One was a familiar silver Infinity, and one was a van from the local CBS station. Kirk climbed out of his vehicle, and his lean body jogged to the front door. Agent Holt answered when he knocked. The crew of the van was unloading equipment.

"Hello, Mr. Mahoney," Marcus said.

Kirk greeted all of us and I asked, "What are you doing here?"

"Heard the call on the scanner. What are you doing here?"

I nodded to Betty Ann and the baby. "We have a doctor's

appointment."

Betty Ann turned to me as she held Maddie tighter. "Are you going to take her away?" Tears ran down her cheeks as she asked me the question.

"I'm afraid that is going to be up to my superiors. I'm going to do everything I can not to have that happen. I would feel better if there was somewhere else you could stay for a while. Do you have a friend or someone who you stay with until this calms down? That would really help me convince my bosses you're looking out for her."

Maddie looked at me and said, "Ba! Na! Goot," as Betty Ann and Marcus looked at each other.

Marcus said, "We are going to stay at an Extended Stay hotel near I-65 for the foreseeable future. I've booked us a suite and will get us packed while y'all visit the doctor." He reached over and stroked Maddie's soft, curly hair. "Please believe me when I say that my family's safety is the most important thing."

I nodded. "I'm going to do everything I can to keep her with you."

The CBS crew knocked on the door. Marcus said, "I'll handle it," and stepped outside.

Kirk asked Agent Holt if we could see the letter. She shrugged. "It's bagged for evidence and I can't let you touch it. We are going to try to get prints off it. But here." She reached into a pocket and took out her phone. She pulled up a photo of the letter. Kirk and I bent over her phone to read it.

This one was different. The letters in the past had been formal, and typed, with few errors and a clear message that sounded like a treatise. This one was hand-written in small capital letters, neatly printed on a sheet of notebook paper.

Boy-
You will never be Mayer of this city. I will make sure you die before that happens. You and your wife are goin to get blowed up sky high. They will not even find your body. Drop out now and you might live. Good by.

"This one is different," I stated.

"Indeed." Agent Holt said. "It's likely the writer doesn't have a computer, nor is he very tech-savvy. The letter was postmarked Birmingham. We have a couple of suspects we are rounding up."

"Joe-Bob Gaines?" I asked.

She smiled. "He's one for sure."

I checked my watch and told Betty Ann we needed to leave.

"Did you see the article in the paper this morning?" Kirk asked me.

"I haven't had a second to look, but I will." I got a smile for that.

I loaded Betty Ann and Maddie into my car and we headed for downtown to MidCity Pediatrics at the University of Alabama-Birmingham. I finally found a place to park and we made our way to the office. Betty Ann and Marcus had chosen Dr. Thomas Andrews as their doctor. He had been in practice for years and years, and Betty Ann said he'd been Tameka's doctor as well, years ago. I had numerous clients over the years who had seen him.

We sat in the waiting room as Maddie crawled around the play area filled with toys. Betty Ann watched her as I filled out paperwork, and when that was done, I pulled up the <u>Birmingham News</u> app on my phone. I could see the front page on the app, and the small article on the front page with the byline Kirk Mahoney.

LOCAL BUSINESSMAN'S WIFE MISSING

Patricia Alsbrook, wife of CEO James Alsbrook of Alsbrook Coal Inc., has not been seen since Friday evening. Her grown son, Jason Alsbrook, was killed in the bombing January 8 at the office of mayoral candidate Marcus Freedman. It is believed she is with a friend and is unharmed.

Kirk went on to state that the Alsbrooks were mourning their son who was buried in a private ceremony on January 14. He asked anyone who had information on Patricia's whereabouts to please call Alsbrook Coal. It was a very neutral article, and gave no indication of what was to come next weekend. I couldn't wait for Sunday.

Dr. Andrews's nurse came in and gathered us. She weighed Maddie and measured her height, then we waited in a room for the doctor. Dr. Andrews was about sixty years old, with snowy gray hair and bright blue eyes. He smiled, always, and his face bore small wrinkles to prove that fact. He lit up when he saw Maddie and greeted me and Betty Ann.

Betty Ann gave a bit of history, wiping away tears as she told him about Tameka. He listened sympathetically and asked what her drug of choice had been. I told him it was believed to be opioids, but with addicts there was likely to be more than one. Maddie hadn't tested positive for drugs at birth or we would have been called.

"Well, let's take a little look at you, Cutie-pie." He picked her up and laid her on the examination table. He listened to her heart and lungs and asked about her sleep schedule and crawling. Betty Ann said she was pulling up and he agreed walking would be soon. She was moving off formula and onto more solid baby foods, and had a love for peas, it seemed.

"I don't see any obvious developmental delays at this point," Dr. Andrews said. "We'll keep an eye out in future checks."

"Ca!" Maddie said.

"Really? Tell me about it," Dr. Andrews said as he handed Maddie back to Betty Ann. He said he'd follow up in a year, then added she should call him with any problems. Betty Ann and I checked out and headed south. I called Jessica, my unit secretary, and asked to see Mac as soon as he had a second. Betty Ann checked her phone in the car and gave me directions to an Extended Stay hotel in Homewood off I-65.

I followed her to her room, where Marcus was unpacking. He had a pack and play set up in the bedroom, as well as a changing table with diapers and several toys. Betty Ann placed Maddie in the pack and play, where she grabbed a stuffed frog and said, "Dee."

Betty Ann closed the door and invited me to join her on the couch. I checked my watch and said I had a second. Marcus was hanging up his suits in the bedroom.

"When will we know if she can stay?" Betty Ann asked.

"I called and set up a meeting with my boss. Hopefully, I can talk to him this afternoon and get this resolved. As long as you are staying here, I don't see a problem."

"I just want this to be over, and my family to be safe."

"Me, too." My phone dinged and the message showed from Jessica. Mac could see me in half an hour, so I said my goodbyes to the Freedmans and headed for the office.

Chapter Nineteen

I parked in the lot in the back and made my way to Mac's office. He was finishing up with another member of my unit and I waited while they wound things up. He motioned me in.

"I haven't seen much of you lately," he stated. "How are things going with LaReesa?"

"Fine. Trying to get her a little caught up in school, but she's adjusting."

"And you?"

"Me?"

"Parenting is a big change. How are you and Grant adjusting?"

"We're fine," I lied. "Things are going well."

"So what did you need to see me about?"

I reviewed the events of this week, about Priscilla Alsbrook's vanishing and what happened this morning. I told him about the letter, and the FBI, and the Freedmans moving to a hotel. "They are really wanting to keep Maddie with them," I concluded.

"Do you think she's safe?"

"I do, really. They're staying at a hotel until all this blows over, and the FBI is working on tracking down the person who made the threat. He's hired a security team. Maddie is bonding with both of them, and the very thought of sending her away puts Betty Ann in tears. I think Maddie is okay."

"You will monitor the situation with the FBI and keep me informed. If the threats increase, we will have to find a new placement."

"I know. I will. Thanks, Mac."

I went back to my cubicle and noted Russell was out. I checked my watch. I had an hour until I had to pick up Reese at school, then I had an appointment in the evening with one of my families. My phone rang. It was my gynecologist's office, reminding me that LaReesa had an appointment on Thursday after school. I filled out a sick leave form for Mac, explaining in writing that Reese had a doctor's appointment in the afternoon. I called Betty Ann with the good news, then did some filing and went to pick Reese up at school.

The assistant principal met me at the car and asked me to follow her to her office. I did, worried about what she was about to tell me. LaReesa was already in the office, in a chair in front of the desk, arms crossed, and she looked fit to explode.

Uh oh, I thought.

Mrs. Roper sat behind her desk and gestured for me to sit down. "We've had a little issue today with LaReesa's temper," she began. "In the restroom, she and a girl got into a conflict about something, and LaReesa threatened her. We cannot have this type of behavior, as I have explained to LaReesa."

"I shoulda punched the bitch," LaReesa said.

"That's enough, Reese," I said.

"We are starting with this conference as the sole consequence for now, but if this becomes a pattern, we will have to move to more severe measures, like suspension, or alternative school."

"I understand. Reese, you remember that goal you have after high school? To go to cosmetology school?"

"Yeah."

"They will not let you in if you have severe problems with your behavior. And do you remember what Judge Myer said, if you want to stay with me? If you don't want to, let me know now, and I can find you a foster home, or a group home."

That earned me a nervous glance. "No, I want to stay with you."

"Then you are going to have to walk away from any conflict, you hear me? Just walk away. If you respond, you give them power over your situation and put your goals at risk."

Reese nodded. I added, "And if someone is bothering you, I'm sure Ms. Roper will listen and help you handle it."

Ms. Roper added, "I'd be happy to help."

I stood up and thanked her, and made sure she had my cell number in case of other problems. Reese followed me out to the car. I could tell she was still upset as she fastened her seat belt. As we pulled out of the parking lot, I asked, "So what happened?"

"This bitch named MacKenzie Thorne. Called me a stupid n-word, and said my mother was a whore. She acts like she's real rich and better than everybody. I told her I was gonna shoot her in the face. I wanna fuckin' kill her. How could she know about my mamma? I wonder if Sharonda told her. Now I wanna kill both of them."

"Wait, wait, wait. You are making a whole lot of assumptions. Do you think Sharonda would be friends with someone like MacKenzie? Or talk about your business behind your back?"

"No."

"I think calling someone's mother a whore is a pretty common insult. Then when you reacted, you proved her right."

"I didn't think about that."

"Don't go accusing Sharonda of something without any evidence. If you are concerned, talk to her about it. Calmly."

"Can I have my phone back?"

"Tomorrow morning."

That got me a frustrated sigh. I made up for it by offering pizza for dinner, which cheered her up a bit. She sat at the dining room table and started her homework. I went to my appointment with my clients from work, who had been court ordered to therapy. The in-home therapist met me there, and had good progress to report. We agreed to continue the current plan and I arrived home about seven thirty. Grant and Reese were at the dining room table. Grant was on a laptop while Reese worked on a worksheet.

"Hey," I greeted them both. "What are we working on?"

"Social Studies," Reese answered.

"I installed a security system at the office. Come see." He held an arm out to me and placed it around my waist as I joined him behind the table. The camera was black and white but the picture was really clear. It was a distinct shot of the cash register and the area behind the counter at his shop. He hit a button on the computer and the view changed to a different section of the store, then another. "I've had more money go missing from the register, so I put these in to get some answers. It's never very much money, but someone is taking it."

"Tol' you I din' steal it," Reese muttered under her breath.

"LaReesa said we are ordering pizza for dinner?" Grant asked.

"Yeah, she's had kinda a rough day, and mine has been long, too. I'm going to call Dad and see if he wants to join us."

"Hell yeah!" Reese declared.

I dialed Dad's number on my phone and he picked up after several rings. I asked him if he wanted to come over for dinner and he declined. "Sorry, kiddo, I'm in the middle of a big project over here. I turned your brother's room into an office years ago, you know? The stuff in there has gotten really out of control. I'm cleaning it out. I don't know why I kept most of this stuff anyway. Lots of books and papers I don't need."

I offered to bring him a pizza and he said he had something for dinner. I told him Reese and I would stop by tomorrow after school and he said he'd enjoy that. After supper, at bedtime, I checked in with LaReesa.

"You feeling better?" I asked.

"Yeah, I'm gonna talk to Shar tomorrow but I don't think she started this."

"I don't either. And you are going to ignore MacKenzie, right?"

"As much as I can."

That was all I could hope for.

The next morning, I gave the phone back to Reese with the understanding that I would take it away again if her behavior didn't stay on course. I also explained that I would need the pass code, and it had to stay as it was set. I had set it to the month and date of her birthday, 0729. She took it from me and opened it immediately.

"Where my contacts?" she asked.

"I deleted them. They appeared to be all men and boys, and we need to get your mind focused on other things."

I dropped Reese off as usual and anxiously watched my phone all day for a call from Mrs. Roper. I didn't hear anything from her and was thankful for that. After work I picked Reese up from school, and she and Sharonda were giggling at the flagpole when I pulled up.

"How was your day?" I asked as she strapped in.

"Good. MacKenzie avoided me all day. I think she scared of me."

"And you talked to Sharonda?"

"I tol' her what happened. She so mad at MacKenzie. She din' tell her nothing. I think you right, she just said that and I got upset."

"She struck a nerve." I headed for Dad's house, glad this eighth-grade crisis had been resolved, at least for now. I had memories of my eighth-grade year being similar. Groups of girls ganging up against other groups of girls loaded with lots of drama. Royanne and I stuck together through it all and we had each other's back. I hoped Sharonda was going to be that kind of friend. It seemed so.

I said, "Listen, tomorrow after school you have a doctor's appointment."

"For what? I ain't sick."

"You are a young lady and a yearly gynecologist appointment is important to make sure you are healthy, especially considering your history."

"He gon' look at my hoo ha?"

I chuckled. "*She* is going to do an exam. Have you had one of those before?"

"No. I don't wanna go."

"I promise you, you won't die of embarrassment. It's never

fatal."

I pulled into Dad's driveway with that statement. It was a clear, cool day and the view of Jones Valley behind the nineteen-sixties, ranch-style house was especially beautiful.

"Whoa…" LaReesa muttered. "This where he live?"

"It is. This is the house I grew up in."

We made our way through the front door as I called to Dad. I glanced around, trying to see the house as Reese would see it, for the first time. The furniture was very outdated, and little had changed since my Mom died eighteen years ago. The walls were a creamy white, and the carpet a stained beige. I knew it was all old, and loved it anyway. It was home.

LaReesa was studying everything around her with interest. Dad called to us from the bedrooms down the hallway. I led LaReesa to where he was and they greeted each other enthusiastically.

"This room used to be my brother's," I explained. The room was painted blue-gray. Chris's bunk beds were long gone, but the dresser and desk remained. At the moment they were covered in papers and boxes. "What's all this?" I asked Dad.

"I need some more storage space, and all this stuff has been in here for years. I'm cleaning out."

I opened a shoe box on the desk, only to discover my school pictures from all my years of elementary and high school. I tried to slam the lid back on the box but LaReesa caught my hand before I could.

"Whaa? Lemma see!" she squealed.

"Oh, crap," I muttered.

She dug through the pictures while laughing hysterically. My third-grade one was especially bad, with a sharp, bob haircut and hideous dark green outfit. At the bottom of the box was a picture of a pretty woman with blond hair, holding a baby about a year old.

"Is dis you?" she asked, picking up the photo.

"It is. That's me and my mom."

"Where she at now?"

"She died when I was thirteen. Your age," I realized.

"How she die?"

"Breast cancer."

My father had gone very quiet and I turned to him. His expression was sad but he gave me a small smile. "She was a very special person."

"What her name was?' Reese asked.

"Carolyn," Dad said. "Will you take that box of pictures to

your house?"

"Sure. What is all this stuff?"

"Most of it I am recycling. Look," he said, pulling an old box to him. "I kept everything." He opened the box to reveal stacks of phone books from my elementary years. "Remember phone books? Why I kept these, I have no idea."

"What's a phone book?" Reese asked.

"Many years ago, if you wanted to know someone's phone number, you looked it up here in one of these books." I picked one up from over fifteen years ago and thumbed through it. "Hmm," I muttered, flipping through to "Conover". Christopher and Carolyn, it read, and this address on South Shades Crest Road. I pointed it out to Reese. "See?" I flipped again to Fayard on Rushmore Way. "And this was my best friend's house. Her parents still live there." Roy and Anne would be there forever, I hoped.

I suddenly had a thought, and checked the front of the thick book. It was for all of the Birmingham metro area for that year. I turned to the C's again and scanned for Cushman. There were a number of them, maybe twenty. What were Ronald's parent's names? Bernard? And? I checked the list. There they were: Bernard and Penelope Cushman. They had an address in East Birmingham, near the area of Roebuck. Little John Lane was the address.

"Hey, Dad, you don't mind if I tear this page out of this book, do you?"

"I don't care. They are going to be recycled. Why?"

"It's something for one of my cases, don't worry about it." I carefully tore the page out of the book and slipped it in my purse.

Reese had left the room and was studying the photographs in frames that lined Dad's hallway. They were all black and white photos of my grandparents and one blurry one of my great-grandparents. I explained it all to Reese, about who they were and how we were related.

"What happened to my Grandma's house?" she asked.

"Did she own it?"

"Yeah, she say once she and Grandpa bought it, before he died."

"Did your grandmother have a will?"

"I dunno."

"I would imagine it's going to go to your mama and your aunt, when they get out of jail."

"Huh. They jus' gonna sell all the stuff and buy drugs."

I didn't know what to say to that. She was probably right. "Do you want to go over there this weekend? Get pictures or anything?"

"Can we? It's probably already been broke into, and all the stuff stolen."

"We can go see."

She gave me a smile for that.

Chapter Twenty

Thursday, I picked up Reese a little early from school to give us plenty of time to get to the doctor. The doctor's office was in Hoover in an area known as Riverchase. I'd seen Dr. Balasaro since my late teens, and liked the way that she interacted with her patients.

I filled out paperwork for Reese while she played on her phone. She and Sharonda were into TikTok and she laughed at the various videos people had posted. I went back with her when she was called.

The nurse took her height and weight and asked her to take everything off and change into a gown. Then Reese got a little shy.

"Everything?"

"Yes, dear, everything. She has seen it all before."

I waited outside while Dr. Balasaro did the exam. She called me back in after it was over, and LaReesa was dressed. "Everything went well. She's had a few sexual partners, so I did a pregnancy test that was negative and I want to do an HIV test. I think the HPV vaccine is in order as well."

How many partners? I was dying to ask, but I kept my mouth shut. Maybe it wasn't my business.

"What's an HPV vaccine?" Reese asked.

"HPV is a virus that is linked to different types of cancer, correct?" I asked the doctor.

"Correct. HPV is very common, and the vaccine prevents the most severe types that have been linked to cancer. It's actually two shots—"

"Shots! I don't want any shots!" LaReesa practically screamed.

I answered her. "Listen. If you can survive months on your own, on the street, you can survive two needle sticks."

Dr. Balasaro added, "And what about birth control?"

I looked at Reese. "I hope we are not going to be having sex with anyone right now, but what do you think?"

"I'm not, but the doc says it'll help with my monthlies."

"Ok, then let's do that."

We checked out with a prescription and an appointment to come back for a second shot. LaReesa handled the first shot well and finally understood the necessity of it. Once in the car and strapped in, I asked what she thought of her first exam.

"She nice, the doc."

"I agree."

"She din' say much when I told her about last year. About my partners. I mean she wasn't all judge-y."

"That's nice to hear." Please keep talking, I thought.

She looked embarrassed, avoiding eye contact with me and fiddling with her seat belt. Her gaze was on her shoes. "He pimped me out," she almost whispered.

My stomach turned. "Who's he?"

"The guy I was staying with. He'd get money from his friends and I'd have to do them. Sometimes it wasn't just sex, like I'd have to like…suck them off."

"Good God, Reese."

"I had to. I needed a place to stay. I din' want to go to foster care."

"I know, I'm not upset with you. That really sucks that you had to go through that at thirteen years old."

She nodded. "I know."

I turned to her. "What he did to you was horrible, and also illegal. It's child abuse. If you want to press charges against him, I can help make that happen."

She thought about that for a second. "Nah," she said. "It was horrible, but I did have a place to sleep that wasn't on the street."

"What was his name?"

"Roderick."

"Last name?"

"I dunno."

She was lying, but I let it slide. "Did you tell all this to the doctor?" I wondered if Balasaro or her nurse was going to call my office.

"Not his name. She said she could report this and have him punished, just like you said. I tol' her not to. I don' wanna have to go through it all again."

"Well, if in the future you change your mind, let me know. Do you have homework?"

"A little, in Science. Can Sharonda come spend the night tomorrow?"

"That sounds like a great idea."

She brightened at that. "Can we rent movies? And order Chinese food?"

"Sure, that would be fun."

"Cool!" She pulled out her phone and began to text frantically. Suddenly, she was thirteen again, and not a recovering teenage prostitute. I headed home, a small fire of anger raging in my gut. I wanted to go after whoever Roderick was, and hard. Put him in prison. But I couldn't do that without Reese's testimony. Maybe she just needed time to think about it. In the meantime, I should think about a therapist for her.

After we got home from the doctor, I called Cheryl Fowler to confirm things with her. She answered after the first ring.

"Hey!"

"Hi Cheryl. I'm calling on behalf of LaReesa, who would like Sharonda to come over tomorrow and spend the night?" I could hear Reese pacing in the next room and listening to every word. I walked back to my room and shut the door.

"Tomorrow is Friday, so they shouldn't have any homework. I don't have a problem with that."

"Thanks. We'll take good care of her, I promise. Oh, and I wanted to ask you about something. When Reese came home from your house last weekend, she had a bunch of clothes with her that she said Sharonda gave her. I wanted to make sure you knew about it and were okay with it?"

"Oh yeah. See…" I heard Cheryl shut a door behind her. "Shar was overweight last year. Really overweight, and the other kids gave her hell about it. She took it upon herself to do something about it, and starting eating healthy and exercising. Those clothes were things she had when she was heavier. I'm fine with Reese having them."

"Oh, I'm glad she lost the weight."

"The other kids were horrible, calling her fat ass and worse."

"God, middle school. What a nightmare."

Cheryl laughed. "Right? Wouldn't go back for a billion dollars."

"Me neither."

I told Cheryl I'd pick Sharonda and Reese up tomorrow from school and we agreed to get together soon. When I opened the door to my bedroom, LaReesa had her head up against the door and fell backwards, nearly landing on her butt. I shot her a look.

"What she say? Can Sharonda spend the night?"

"Nobody's coming over if you don't stop listening to my conversations."

"But it's about me."But it's my conversation."

"What she say?" Reese was practically bouncing up and down now, waiting for an answer.

"She said yes and I'm going to pick you both up at school tomorrow."

"Yay!" Reese shouted.

"Listen if you are having a guest tomorrow, you should straighten your room. Are you going to sleep in there? The both of you?"

"Can we sleep on the floor of the living room? And watch movies?"

The floor was carpeted, but not with anything thick. "That doesn't sound comfortable." I had a thought. "Wait," I said to her. My laundry room was off the carport and contained some shelves where I stored things, mostly camping equipment. Reese followed me and watched while I found the queen-sized air mattress.

"There," I said, handing her the box.

"Awesome!"

"It needs to be cleaned up a bit, after you are done with your room. And your homework."

Grant got home a little after five and Reese excitedly told him about the plans for tomorrow. He didn't seem too happy about it, so I followed him back to our room where he was changing clothes. I closed the door behind us.

"You are not okay with Sharonda spending the night?"

"I just wish you had talked to me about it before you set everything up."

"I didn't realize this had to be decided by committee. It's one girl spending the night."

"I'm not a committee. But I do live here, in case you've forgotten."

"What the hell is the matter with you?"

"Me? You have no consideration for me. You just do what you do with no thought of me whatsoever. I feel like I'm just a renter here."

That stopped me cold. Was he right? I'd brought LaReesa home in the middle of the night with no discussion with him at all. And today I'd done it again, made a decision without him. Still, I was an adult and didn't need his permission. I didn't say anything. I felt the urge to apologize, but I didn't need to. I hadn't done anything wrong. Now I was pissed.

"I've had a very rough day," he said. "I was hoping for a quiet, stress-free weekend."

"What happened?"

"I'll show you. Come on."

I followed him to the office where he booted his laptop. "Remember I said I'd installed cameras in the shop? To track the money that's gone missing?"

"Yes. You thought it was LaReesa that stole it."

"I know. It wasn't her."

I looked at the screen, where a black and white shot of the interior of High Tech was displayed. Grant had worked so hard the past few years, getting the shop up and running and developing a client base. I hated to hear something was threatening that.

He pushed a few buttons on the laptop and I could see an overhead view of his check-out counter, where the cash register stood along with some displays. Nothing happened for a minute or so, then I saw Regina, his employee, approach the register. She looked over her shoulder and around her, subtly, and opened the drawer. She slid her hand in and took some of the money there and slid it into her pocket.

Chapter Twenty One

"Damn!" I exclaimed. "Seriously? That bitch!"

Grant gave a wry smile. "My thoughts exactly. I don't ever keep that much in the register, and to be real honest, I don't really track it that carefully, but it seems she's been at this a long while. I think she's taken about seven hundred dollars from me."

Grant had told me about his history with Regina. She had come into High Tech just before we met last summer, her five-year-old son in tow and on the run from her abusive husband. She had dropped out of high school and had few skills. He had hired her, trained her in basic computer repair, and paid her above minimum wage. She owed everything to him, and this is what she does? I was so mad.

"I went by the Hoover Police Department on the way home and filed a report with a Detective Hale. He's coming by the shop on Monday. I pressed charges and she's going to be arrested. And fired, of course."

"What's her son's name?"

"Dylan."

"And he's what? About five now?"

"I think so."

"I wonder who he'll live with?"

"According to Regina, she got full custody, so I don't know."

"I'm sorry this happened."

"You just can't trust anybody."

I looked at the floor. *Not even me*, I thought.

Friday, I worked until it was time to pick up the girls. I hadn't heard anything from Kirk in days, and called him on the way to the school.

"Hey you, what's going on?"

"I'm putting the final edits on the story. It'll be in Sunday's paper. I told you it's the lead story, right?"

"You did. Congratulations."

"I've also been trying to track down some friends and acquaintances of Ronald Cushman. I tracked down two of his army buddies, but no one has heard from him."

"Oh! That reminds me…hang on." I pulled over and got out the phone book page I'd taken from Dad's house earlier in the week. "I found an address for Ronald's parents, Bernard and Penelope Cushman. It's northeast of here, in Roebuck." I read him the address. "This is fifteen or twenty years old though. It doesn't look like Ronald has any siblings, so he probably inherited the house, assuming his parents are dead."

"And probably sold it. I'll look and see. Thanks."

We disconnected as I pulled into the carpool line at Goodwin Middle. The girls were there, and Sharonda was holding her book bag as well as a small overnight case. They piled into the back seat and talked nonstop all the way home.

LaReesa had cleaned her room as asked, and cleaned and inflated the air mattress. The girls placed it in the living room in front of the television while I found some blankets for it. They both typed away on their cell phones as the TV played. I left them to it.

The evening went smoothly. The girls streamed two movies with superheroes I had no interest in seeing. I read in my room and Grant stayed in the office, typing something. I wandered out to check on the girls, who were doing just fine, thank you, and went to Grant in the office. He was working busily on his laptop.

I massaged his shoulders. "What are you doing?" I asked.

"Typing up a report for the police, about Regina."

"What's her last name?"

"Maynard. Why?"

"I just have a feeling this is going to land in my unit. I want to be on the lookout."

"She'll probably find a friend to take her."

"I hope so."

At midnight the girls were sound asleep. I turned off the TV and went to bed. Saturday morning Grant and I took the girls to Cracker Barrel for breakfast and dropped Sharonda off at home. She thanked both of us repeatedly and said she had a great time. On the way home I asked Reese, "Did you have fun?"

"Oh my God that was so much fun. Thanks for lettin' me have her sleep over."

"You're welcome. We'll have to do that again sometime. Do you want to go by your grandmother's house?" I had mentioned this to Grant this morning and he had offered the use of his van.

"Sure."

I gave Grant directions to the house in Midfield. When we pulled up, it looked much as it had the last time I had seen it, in the fall, except the toys were missing off the front porch and one of the shutters was hanging loose.

"I wonder if the key still there," LaReesa said. She got out of the van and went to the front porch. She reached under one of the rotting wooden steps and pulled off a piece of duct tape. Shining silver on the back of the tape was a key. She used it to open the front door.

"Wait," Grant said. "Let me go first."

We waited on the porch while he walked through the house and gave us the okay to come in. It was freezing inside as LaReesa looked around. I followed her. She went back to her old bedroom, which she had shared with her small cousins, DeCaria and DeCora, who had been ten and six the last time I saw them. They were both in foster care now.

LaReesa looked in the closet and it was empty. She went across the hall to what had been her grandmother's bedroom. The bed was still there, but the sheets and blankets had been removed. There was a yellow stain in the middle of the mattress. Her closet was full of her grandma's clothes, mostly. Reese opened the nightstand next to the left side of the bed and looked in the drawer.

"All her pills gone."

"They likely went to the hospital with her when she went there."

"Oh, yeah."

Reese turned to a dresser in front of the bed. It was covered in framed photos, and she called me over. There was a gold frame around a 4 x 6 photo of two black teen girls sitting close together on a bench, arms around each other and big goofy smiles on their faces. Reese pointed to the girl on the right. "Thas' my mamma. An' her sister, a buncha years ago."

"She's pretty."

Reese shrugged. "Used to be. 'Fore the drugs got her." She gestured to another photo, a 5 x 7 wedding picture in another gold frame. From the look of the veil and the length of the dress, it looked to be from the mid-nineteen sixties. A lovely bride stood next to a handsome man in a suit as they smiled for the camera. "Thas' my grandma, and my granddad on they wedding day." The smiling woman looked nothing like the elderly, angry woman I had met last year. There were a few pictures of Reese, too, in elementary school, and a couple of baby pictures of her cousins.

"Did you know your granddad?"

"Yeah, he died of a heart attack when I was eight. He was nice."

"Do you want to take these photos?"

"Yeah, if I can."

Grant went out to the van and grabbed a small empty box that had once held a router. We placed the photos in the box as Reese looked around some more. She checked the last bedroom that had belonged to DeCameron, her youngest cousin, who was about two years old now. Everything was cleaned out of that one, too. I hoped Russell, who was the social worker who had placed them in foster care, had gotten their stuff. Reese didn't seem to want anything else in the house so we headed home. LaReesa was quiet on the way and I wondered what she was feeling.

"You okay?" I asked.

"Uh-huh. I feel like I should miss her more. But I don't, because we never really got along."

"There's no wrong way to grieve for someone."

LaReesa was quiet and spent much of the day alone. I could hardly wait for the next day. Sunday morning, I fetched the newspaper from the driveway. The *News* had gone almost totally digital in recent years but still printed the paper on Sundays, their busiest day. I kept up my subscription mostly because I liked to peruse it with a cup of coffee on Sunday mornings. Kirk's article was the lead story on the front page, the headline reading: "HE WAS WARNED". The byline was Kirk Mahoney, staff writer. He'd found a photo of James, one with him in a suit like Corporate execs take for their businesses. He was in a light gray suit, gray hair neatly combed, and a red tie knotted at his neck. The picture filled most of the page above the fold.

The article was divided into sections, and next to each section were more, smaller photos. The first was the one of Benjamin Burke we'd seen at his mother's house, a thin young man with spiky hair, dressed in jeans and no shirt, standing next to an unlit bonfire. I read on.

"First, Benjamin Burke

Benjamin Burke, known as B.B. to friends and family, descends from a family of miners. His grandfather worked in the mines for several decades, then his father. They supported their families and took pride in their work. BB wanted to do the same. He began working at the Warm Creek Mine in Shelby County when he was twenty. He worked there for four years, earning enough money to purchase a trailer and buy his own truck. When he was twenty-four, he was killed when a spark from an older lamp set off a methane explosion. He died with five other miners that day.

James Alsbrook, owner and CEO of Alsbrook Mining Company, was warned. His Warm Creek Mine was cited six months before the disaster because the equipment they were using needed replacing. Alsbrook Mining Company was fined, but no evidence has been found to show he has updated his equipment. The Warm Creek Mine remains open."

Next, Kirk had tracked down Chad Davenport's senior picture from high school. A lump formed in my throat as a studied it. He still had the red hair and freckles and stared at the camera with no smile.
"Second, Chad Davenport
Little Chad Davenport spent his childhood in chaos. His father was schizophrenic, and his mother left when he was a baby. He was reared in the foster care system, and not much else is known about his short life. He did what a lot of young men do after he graduated from high school: he got a job. He began working at the Green Valley Mine in North Jefferson County when he was eighteen. He was killed instantly seven months later when an explosion rocked the mine.
James Alsbrook was warned. The mine was cited three months before Chad's death for using explosives that were degenerated and unfit for use. They were used anyway. Alsbrook Mining Company was cited and fined, but The Green Valley Mine remains open."

Glen Coyne was a strapping lad, I noted. Strong and capable-looking. The snapshot of him was in a white tee and overalls, bending over the engine of an antique truck as he smiled for the camera.
"Third, Glen Coyne
Glen was all boy, his mother said. As a child, he loved to take his toys apart and put them back together. His father, Wendell "Flip" Coyne, owns Coyne's Fireworks here in Jefferson County and hoped his son would take over the business one day. Glen wanted to work on his own for a while first, and got a job at The Rock Creek Mine in north Jefferson County. He loved to fish and was saving for a boat, and a truck to tow it. He was severely injured when the rock roof collapsed at the mine. He was hospitalized at UAB but it was soon discovered that he would not recover. His parents had to discontinue life support.
James Alsbrook was warned. The Mine Safety and Health Administration noted the ceiling was unsupported and could collapse. Alsbrook Mining Company was fined after the accident and the Rock Creek mine was closed."

Timothy Kramer was a blond kid who looked young for his age. He stood next to a Christmas tree in the next photo, dressed in an oversized sweater.

"*Fourth, Timothy Kramer*

Timothy and his family lived in Cullman, and Timothy went to work for Alsbrook Mining after getting an Associate's degree in Business after high school. His parents had six children total, and Timothy was the youngest. They were unable to provide more education for him, and jobs were scarce during the recession. He was hired at the Double Creek Mine and he was glad to have the work. He didn't expect to love mining, but he did. He was proud of the income he could bring to his elderly parents every month. He was killed after an explosion in the mine. Once again, James Alsbrook had been warned by the Federal Government that the explosion might happen due to poor ventilation, and no action was taken. Double Creek Mine remains open."

Next, Kirk had used the photo we'd seen at Gayle Parks' house, the one with him holding his diploma from Johnson High School.

"*Fifth, Ronnie Parks*

Ronnie Parks was a superstar. Born to a single, black teenage mother in Wylam, he avoided all the things that often derail young black men in his neighborhood; drugs, gangs, and crime. He got a job in high school at a fast food restaurant and was on track to become a manager when he got offered a job at the Warm Creek Mine. He took it because it paid better. He'd worked there four months when the explosion happened. He was killed instantly, as he was standing next to our first fatality, Benjamin Burke.

It took all of Ronnie's mother's savings, and some borrowed money, to lay him to rest. Benjamin Burke's mother, Dana, was a friend of Ronnie's mother. Despite her own emotional devastation, she started an organization called The Mourned Miners to help with burial costs after mining disasters. She raises money at events yearly and will accept donations for those who want to help. Her website is mournedminersofalabama.com.

James Alsbrook of Alsbrook Mining was warned, multiple times. These are just a few of the young men that have died at his facilities. There are additional young men with hopes and dreams that will never be fulfilled. How many more have to die? James

Alsbrook lost his son Jason nearly three weeks ago in the explosion at Marcus Freedman's office. One has to wonder if the bomber was out for revenge. Or justice."

It was a good article, painting James as a villain and pointing out all of his selfish decisions. I wondered what he was thinking this morning. I pulled out my cell and called Kirk.

"Hey, great article."

"Let me call you back."

Twenty minutes later my phone rang. "Sorry, I was checking in at a hotel."

"A hotel?"

"Yeah, kinda close to you, near the Galleria. Can you come here and I'll explain?"

"Where are you?"

He told me the name of the big chain hotel that was about ten minutes away, and his room number. I told Grant and Reese I had to step out for a minute and sped my Honda there. I knocked on the door of the room number he had given me and he opened the door.

"Come on in," he said. He was unpacking a number of pastel-colored oxfords from a large hanging bag.

"What's going on?"

He pulled his cell phone from his pocket. "Listen."

Chapter Twenty Two

He put it on speakerphone and pressed play. I heard James Alsbrook's voice. He started calmly. "Mr. Mahoney. You have printed an article today in the *News* which I do not appreciate. You did not get a comment from me or present my side of the story at all."

I noted James was getting louder. "You will be hearing from my attorneys immediately. I don't know who the *fuck* you think you are but I am going to sue you and your *fucking* paper into the next century!"

He was really shouting now. "You will not have a *fucking* dime when I'm through with you! And God help you if I see you on the street. I will kill you!" The message ended with a click.

Kirk said, "It was that last statement that made my editors tell me to go a hotel, temporarily. They want me to be safe, and are footing the bill." He gestured around him. "What do you think? Wanna test out the bed?"

"Kirk--"

"Just dreaming."

"Do you really think he knows where you live?"

"I think it would pretty easy to find out, with a little legwork. There are plenty of people in this hotel, all the time. They have good security. It might be harder to get to me."

"Did you call the police?"

"I did. I filed a police report, but I likely won't be allowed to do much more than that."

"But he threatened you! He said he would kill you."

"If he sees me on the street, yes. You do care."

"I just keep thinking about that antique gun cabinet, and how unstable he is."

Kirk walked toward me and placed his arms around me. "You do care."

"As a friend, of course."

He bent down and gave me little nibbling kisses on my neck. "Nothing more?" he whispered.

I could feel his warm breath on my neck and the strong muscles in his arms. It felt good. It felt exciting. It felt like it could be a new beginning. The room was getting smaller and there seemed to be less air in it. I pushed him away. "Why won't you be able to file a restraining order or something?"

He sighed. "The courts need more than just one idle threat. If you could file a motion every time somebody said, 'I'm going to kill you', the courts would be backed up for decades. Centuries maybe. They just won't do it."

"What about the attorneys at the paper?"

"They are mostly experts in slander and libel and such. But they are looking into it. Let's have some fun." He moved toward me.

I moved toward the door. "I've got to go."

"Because you are tempted."

"I have a family."

"You have a foster child, and a boyfriend."

"Same thing. Take care of yourself."

"I'll walk down with you. I need to get my computer out of my car."

"Did you look into Ronald Cushman's parents? And who owns the house?"

"That's on today's agenda."

We walked together to my car. I asked, "Will you call me when you find something? About the house?"

"Of course." He opened my car door for me and kissed me on the cheek. "Take care of yourself."

I touched his face, gently. "You too. For real."

I drove back to my house and was surprised to see Grant's van was absent. Reese was on the couch, still in her pajamas. "Where's Grant?" I asked.

She shrugged. "Said he had someplace to go. What's for lunch?"

"I could make some sandwiches?"

LaReesa joined me in the kitchen and the two of us made a plate of ham sandwiches and heated up some soup. Grant walked in just as we finished. I offered him a sandwich."No, thanks." He seemed angry.

"You okay? You seem upset about something."

He gave me a forced smile. "Nothing I can't handle."

I was anxious and distracted all day Monday, waiting to hear from Grant about what happened with Regina Maynard. Even Russell noticed. I found time to call a counselor and set up an appointment for LaReesa in February. I wished it was sooner but they had a waiting list. I got home at five and Grant walked in a few minutes later. He looked run over.

I tried to put my arms around him in a hug but he stopped me.

"Can you give me a minute? I just walked in the damn door," he snapped.

"Sorry. What happened today?"

"Regina arrived at work at eight. I called her in my office, sat her down and showed her the security video. She started crying and said she was so sorry. She had an outstanding bill at the pediatrician that she had to pay, so she said. As we were talking, Detective Hale arrived. I explained that she was fired and I was pressing charges. The tears got heavier. Detective Hale arrested her and they left."

"I'm so sorry."

"It gets worse. I thought I'd better check some things considering the circumstances. It seems she's been embezzling funds from my clients as well."

"Oh my God."

"I called a few of them to see if anything was amiss. I think she's been stealing things like passwords from my clients." He buried his head in his hands. "I've got to call every client I have had for the past seven months and see if they are missing anything. God, that's going to be a task."

"Is there anything I can do to help?"

"No," he said. "It's all on me."

I left him to change clothes and made dinner. He was quiet during the meal, and seemed to be barely listening to Reese's stories of eighth-grade life at Goodwin Middle School. After supper he said he was going to the office to start working on straightening out the mess made by Regina. I fell asleep before he came home.

Tuesday, I had home visits all morning. At ten, Kirk called and I stepped outside my client's house to answer his call.

"Hey, beautiful."

"What's going on?"

"I did as much research as I could on that house in Roebuck. It doesn't look like it's been sold recently, so I think we should go check it out today."

I glanced at my calendar. I had home visits scheduled for the rest of the morning. I told Kirk this, and asked him if I could meet him there at noon. He agreed.

The home visits went fine, and I was thinking about all the reports I had to write this week as I pulled up to the brick house on Little John Lane. The house was small but well-maintained, the winter-brown grass neat and tidy. The house was light red brick and looked to be two stories, with a single-car garage on the first level along with what I presumed to be a basement. A flight of stone steps led to a small portico on the main floor where the front door and the shutters were painted light blue. A large window was next to the door, shielded by thin, lacy curtains.

Kirk's car was already there, and he was sitting in the driver's seat. He joined me on the front portico and kissed me on the cheek.

"Quit," I said.

"Aww."

"Well, here goes," I said, and knocked on the door. I saw the flimsy curtain move in the big window next to the door but no one answered the door. I knocked again, harder, and called out, "Patricia, it's Claire Conover. I just want to talk to you two."

If Patricia didn't live here, the occupants may well be calling the police, I thought. Kirk was scanning the street as I knocked again. The door opened, slowly, and Patricia Alsbrook stood there with Ronald Cushman behind her, his hand on her shoulder.

Patricia Alsbrook looked like a different woman. She was dressed in jeans and a cute sweater, neither of them baggy. Her hair flowed loose and healthy around her face and her color was good. She'd even gained a couple of pounds.

"How did you find us? Come in," Ronald said.

Kirk and I entered the living room, which was filled with a large television, nice leather furniture and a glass and wrought iron coffee table. The table held various clutter, including a box of tissues and two remote controls. "Come back to the kitchen," Ronald said, leading the way. We walked through the living room to a door on the far side, through an elegant dining room to an average-sized kitchen with brown countertops and beige walls. There was a small table for two against a wall, and an elderly black woman sat there, dressed in a blue housecoat and sipping on a mug of something.

"Hello, Susie," she said to me. "Have you come over to play with Ronald?"

I smiled at her. "Yes, ma'am. Thanks for having me over."

Patricia gathered Mrs. Cushman and escorted her back to what I guessed was her bedroom then rejoined us in the kitchen.

"That's my mamma," Ronald said. "She's seventy-two and has severe Dementia. Most of the time she thinks it's 1980. I had full-time care for her until I left my job. Have you called the police or the authorities?" He exchanged a nervous glance with Patricia, and I could feel their collective anxiety.

"We weren't even sure you were here." Kirk said, "So, no."

"Are you going to call them?" Ronald asked.

"Let's just talk for a while," I said. "We just have a few questions." I held on to my cell phone in case things got dangerous. Ronald invited us back to the living room, where he and Patricia sat close together on the couch and Kirk and I sat facing them in the chairs. Ronald held her hand.

"What questions do you have?" Ronald asked. "Patricia and I love each other, and we just want to be together and for her to be divorced from James."

"But Jason..." I said. "Did you kill Jason?"

Ronald's head fell and he looked at his toes. Patricia's eyes filled with tears as he answered. "I did. I did it before I realized...I just wanted revenge. Ronnie was my only son. James just...goes about his day, earning all his money. He doesn't realize how many lives he has destroyed. And he doesn't care. He won't even give anything to the families of the victims. Not even to pay for the funerals. He deserves to suffer like we did."

He took a deep breath and continued, "I worked there for nearly three years before I did anything. I just wanted to see...to be in his house and see...if he was, you know, sorry. If he worried about people when an accident happened. He doesn't. He gets mad about the money he has to pay. Fine, because that's all he has now."

I looked at Patricia, wanting some input from her. Her voice was strong and confident as she said, "You don't know how bad he was. I got beaten one time because I asked him what he wanted for breakfast. He has so much anger. I didn't know life could be different until I met Ronald. He would step in, when James got really out of control. He saved my life a few times. Of course, I wish my son were still here, but Ronald feels really bad about what he did and I have forgiven him. Poor Jason grew up seeing all that." Patricia focused on Kirk. "Are you going to put this in the paper? If you do, we are going to have to run."

I glanced at Kirk, who looked at me and gave a small grin. "No, this doesn't go in the newspaper. Promise."

I could feel the relief in the room. Mrs. Cushman walked through the living room, her neck loaded with Mardi Gras beads as she carried a small stuffed lion. She headed for the kitchen.

"Excuse me," Ronald said, and went after her.

I asked Patricia, "Do you miss the money?"

"That house, and the money, were nothing but a prison for me. I never saw any benefit from it, nor did Jason. James can have it. I just want to be left alone, with Ronald. I love him very much. You know when we realized it? That day we met you at Mo:Mo. When we got home, I was crying and telling Ronald how I couldn't live like this anymore and Jason was supposed to have gotten me out. He cried too, and said he'd fallen in love with me and would give his life to keep me safe. I confessed I loved him too, and we made plans to leave. Of course, we can't go far with his mother the way she is. Anyway, I found a lawyer who will handle my divorce and keep our location secret, so he's going to get served with papers."

"I saw him, the day after you two left. He was really unhinged."

"I can imagine."

"You look so much better."

"I feel so much better, so happy and…free, I guess. And not scared all the time."

Ronald rejoined us, sitting to the left of Patricia and delicately holding her hand. I told them, "You should know James has a private investigator looking for you two. I think if we could find you, there's a good chance he could, too."

Patricia scoffed, "I have no doubt he will show up eventually. He owns everybody."

"Don't worry," Ronald said, "we are prepared." His hand slid deftly between the cushions of the leather couch and pulled out a handgun.

Chapter Twenty Three

It was a big gun, too. I didn't know enough about guns to know what kind it was, but it was big. And it had a silencer attached. Ronald held it loosely and I could see it had a safety, which he clicked off. I saw Kirk tense in the chair next to me.

"We have these hidden all over the house, in case he shows up." Ronald said.

"But your mother…"

He scoffed, "None in her room, of course, and we watch her all the time. She's fine."

I doubted that, but let it go. Ronald focused on Kirk, aiming the gun in his direction. "We will not appear in your newspaper."

"No, no, no, of course not. I said that, it's all off the record."

The muzzle of the gun moved my way. "Who have you told we are here?"

"No one. Honest. My boss doesn't even know I'm here."

Ronald focused back on Kirk for a moment, pointing the gun at his chest. He said he had guns all over the house, so I slid my hand down between the cushion and the side of the chair but I didn't feel anything immediately.

"Get your hand out of there!" Ronald snapped. I put my hand back in my lap. "The problem is, now I don't know what to do with you. I'm not sure I can let you leave."

Patricia had been quiet and demure this whole time, and now she said, "If he learns you know where we are, he will do anything. Offer you piles of money, anything. I'm not sure you could resist."

I could if it meant saving your life, I thought.

"Give Patricia your cell phones." Ronald commanded. I had nearly forgotten it. I picked it up from where I had placed it on the arm of the chair and passed it to Patricia. Kirk did the same. She placed them on the coffee table in front of her.

I could see Ronald thinking, turning things over in his mind. I said, "If you kill us, this gets really complicated. How would you dispose of our bodies?"

Kirk turned to me, wide eyed, "Claire, what the--"

"You'd get caught," I said, "And go to prison for life."

Ronald was still thinking, so I continued. "And Patricia would go for being an accessory to murder. She just gained her freedom, and I don't want to see her go to prison. Do you?"

A loud knock on the door startled us all. Ronald stuffed the gun back in the couch. The door opened and a middle-aged white lady came in, calling "Yoo hoo? Y'all home?" She was dressed in green scrubs and looked to be about sixty. A lanyard around her neck held a card that I couldn't read. The lanyard was purple, and yellow text all over it read, "TOGETHER INSTEAD HOME CARE". She saw us all, sitting there stiffly, and said, "Oh, I'm sorry. Is this a bad time? I just need to check on Penelope and get her vitals…"

Kirk and I practically jumped to our feet. I dove and grabbed our cell phones and handed Kirk his as I said, "No, no. We were winding up." I looked at Ronald. "You have our word, don't worry."

Ronald looked like he was fuming as Kirk caught the door before it closed. We made our way to our cars, quickly. He followed me back to my office and I sat with him for a minute in his Infinity in the parking lot. He was shaking as we sat there.

"God, Claire. God."

"I know."

"I nearly kissed that nurse when she walked in." He picked up my hand. "How are you not shaking? How are you not freaking out?"

"Because if Ronald was going to kill us, he would have done it as soon as he brought out the gun. And that was actually the…fourth time someone has pulled a gun on me. It doesn't get easier, though."

"I hope that never happens again."

"Me, too. You really aren't going to put their story in the paper, are you?"

He was quiet for a moment. "No, I want them to have a chance to start over. And I don't want Ronald coming after me. Or you."

"He may very well do that if we don't keep their location secret."

"I know." We sat in silence again for a minute and I said, "I've got to get back to work."

He was still holding my hand. "Wait. There's something I have to tell you." He faced me. "I've been promoted."

"Oh, congratulations!" I said. "To an editor, or something?"

"No. The guy who reports on all the stuff in the state capital is retiring after forty years on the beat. They've given me his job."

That took second to sink in. "The capital? You mean Montgomery?"

"Yes. I'm moving in two weeks. My condo is on the market."

"Oh," That was a shock. "I'm sorry to see you go."

"Come with me."

"What?"

"Seriously. Come with me. They have a DHS in Montgomery County. The state office is there, too. You could transfer."

"Kirk, I have a house here, and a foster child. I can't just pack up and go."

"You forgot Grant."

"What?"

"Just now, you didn't mention your boyfriend."

"Oh, of course. Him too. I can't just leave. My father is here. Everything."

"It's only an hour south."

"I know."

"Will you think about it?"

"No, Kirk. I'm sorry, but no. I've had a great time working with you for the past, what, seven months now? But I can't give up my life here."

He looked really disappointed, which kind of surprised me. "I'll call you before I leave. I'm going to miss you. I think we could have had something great."

I scrambled out of the car as tears filled my eyes. I didn't want him to see me getting emotional so I hurried over to my car and sat in the driver's seat as he pulled away.

The events of the day had left me an emotional wreck. Between Ronald pulling the gun and the news that Kirk was leaving, I decided I needed some time to think. I checked my calendar back in my office and rescheduled my afternoon appointments. As I was walking toward the back door to the building, a large number of my fellow social workers began streaming toward the door as well, all of them looking panicked.

I tried to stop a girl in my unit, but she ignored me and continued to the parking lot. I spotted Russell and rushed over to him. "What's going on?"

"Code Orange. There's a guy in the lobby with a pistol. The police are on their way. Mac and Dr. Pope are with him. It's that guy that was in the paper on Sunday from the mining company."

"Oh, shit," I said, as I took off for the lobby. The crowd of colleagues parted around me as I ran and entered the lobby from the back hallway.

James was in the middle of the room, surrounded by the hard, plastic chairs people usually waited in, and his back was toward me. Mac was there, his hands in the air, his ever-present cigar missing. My heart raced as I looked at my friends Nancy and Beth, who worked the front desk. They had their arms wrapped around each other. Nancy was shaking and Beth had tears slowly falling down her cheeks. The Director, Dr. Teresa Pope, was calmly talking to James, who was indeed holding a small, silver revolver. "Mr. Alsbrook, if we could just sit down and talk, and you could put the gun away…"

"No!" James shouted. "Where is she?"

"I'm right here, James."

He swung around, quickly, and the barrel of the gun was pointed at my thorax. I braced myself for a gunshot. He held the gun steady. "Where's my wife?"

"She is safe. Put the gun down and we can talk about it."

"No!" he shouted. I saw his finger tighten on the trigger but still no shot.

"Let these people go, James. Your anger is with me, not them."

"Everyone is staying right here until you tell me where my fucking wife is!"

"She's safe. She is where she wants to be."

"She belongs with me!"

"She disagrees." I heard numerous sirens approaching.

He cocked the gun. I quickly said, "James, you aren't going to get away with this. The police are here. If you shoot, you'll go down for murder and you'll never get Priscilla back."

"I've lost everything! Everything! My son is dead, my wife is gone, and the goddamn Board of my company are shutting it down. Because of that stupid article in the paper."

"You've been through a lot." The sirens were right outside the door and I heard car doors slamming. "The police are here. It's time to make a decision." I hoped the bullet would miss my vital organs.

James shook his head and placed the barrel under his chin. I dove behind a row of chairs as the loud bang echoed but I didn't see him pull the trigger.

Chapter Twenty Four

I lay there in a fetal position with my arms around my head on the dusty linoleum floor as police officers rushed in. A buzz echoed in my head, from the loud gunshot. I heard a lot of shouting and radio traffic. Someone touched my leg.

Mac. "Come on, Claire. It's over."

He helped me to my feet. I couldn't help but glance over at James' lifeless body with the hole in his chin and the large pool of blood on the floor behind him. Mac ushered me up to his office on our floor and I sat in a chair, feeling utterly drained.

"You okay?" Mac asked as he handed me a bottled water. "You were very brave."

"Five," I said.

"Five?"

"That's the fifth time someone has pulled a gun on me."

"Yeah, this job is dangerous. I want you to take tomorrow off, unless you have to be in court."

"I don't."

"Then you are to stay home tomorrow and get some rest. Understood?"

"I need to stay busy."

"You can work from home."

I was numb, and nodded.

"When you get back on Thursday, we can talk about why James Alsbrook wanted to kill you."

"Maddie Freedman is his granddaughter. Was. Was his granddaughter."

"I see. I need to get an update on your cases, obviously."

I chuckled. He rose from his chair and looked out the window. "The TV stations are here. You are not to talk to the media. I hope I don't need to remind you of that."

"I know. No comment."

"That's it. Now go home, get some rest. When you get back, we are also going to discuss your friendship with Kirk Mahoney."

My head snapped up in surprise and my mouth dropped open. Mac said, "Word gets around. See you later."

I gathered my laptop from my office and packed what I needed to work from home tomorrow. Russell stopped me on my way out and gave me a hug. "You okay?"

"I didn't see him pull the trigger. I just saw his body afterward."

"You didn't answer my question."

I smiled. "I'll be okay. I think I just need some rest." Assuming I could sleep without seeing the image of James's blood and body on the lobby floor.

I made my way to my car, stopping briefly to glance in the lobby. Nancy and Beth were gone, and a lot of people and police were milling around the room. James's body was gone but the large amount of blood was still there. Cameras were positioned outside by the front door with a team of reporters waiting for Dr. Pope to comment. I snuck out the back door.

I picked Reese up from school fifteen minutes late. She was not shy about reminding me of that fact. "Where the hell you been? I been waitin' forever."

"I know. I'm sorry. It's been a horrid day."

"Yeah, you don't look so good."

"Thanks!"

"Jus' keepin' it real."

"I've really had enough real today."

I remembered to check my phone after I got home, and had one missed call from Grant, and six missed calls from Kirk, including one message from him. "Hey, what the hell happened? Call me."

I hit the button to dial him back and he answered after the first ring. "I'm at your office."

"I'm at home. My boss knows about our friendship and has warned me not to talk to you."

"Friendship? Is that what we have?"

"Yes, Kirk. Friendship."

"Can you tell me what happened, off the record? I can write my piece from the interview Dr. Pope just gave, but I want to know what you saw."

I told Kirk what happened, including that I didn't see James pull the trigger. I had a thought. "James blamed a lot of what happened on your article. How are you feeling?"

"My article told the truth. It's not my fault he can't deal with it."

"He said his Board of Directors was dissolving his company?"

"Yeah, it turns out he owned only forty-seven percent of Alsbrook Mining. The majority of his millions came from selling the other fifty-three percent. I have a call in to the Chairman of the Board, but she has not returned my call yet. Word is they are liquidating, but his death may really slow that down. Gotta go, call you later."

I turned on the local news at four o'clock. The reporter that had covered the bombing a mere three weeks ago was now in front of my office, relaying how James Alsbrook had committed suicide at the Jefferson County DHS office. Dr. Pope spoke from a microphone in front of the front door, explaining that yes, James did have a granddaughter in the custody of the state, but beyond that DHS would have no comment. It was only a matter of time before they linked this to Marcus Freedman and Maddie. I found my cell phone and dialed Marcus' number.

"Hello?"

"Marcus? How are you? Are you and Betty Ann watching the news?"

"I am. Are you okay? Were you there when he…"

"Pulled the trigger? I was. It was horrible. So, I think the news is going to put your stories together and—"

"I just got off the phone with Kirk Mahoney. Gave him the exclusive and permission to tell the whole story."

I gave an ironic laugh. "Of course, he did. Of course, you did. No surprise there."

"He's really kind."

"I know."

"He's moving to Montgomery."

"I know."

"We'd like to move toward adopting Maddie."

"I'm glad to hear that. I'll give you a call next week and we can make plans."

I shut off everything—phone and TV—and went to bed. Grant got home around six and checked on me for a minute. I gave him a short version of what happened and he said he'd get Reese to school in the morning and let me sleep.

I slept until noon-thirty on Wednesday, dragging myself out of bed and vegging on the couch for the rest of the day. I didn't even get out of my pajamas, and got zero work done. I did text Kirk who replied that the next and final article on the James Alsbrook saga would be in the paper Friday.

Thursday morning, I went out to Roebuck and knocked on Ronald and Patricia's door. Patricia opened it, smiling, a spring in her step and an aura of happiness around her. "Oh, hi," she said when she saw me, looking a little guilty. "Are you okay?"

"I'm fine. How are you?"

She invited me into the living room where Ronald sat on the couch. "Don't worry," she said, sitting beside him. "We've gotten rid of the guns. I can't believe he's really gone."

A picture of his bloody body flashed in my head again. "Oh, he is."

"Claire, so many things have been happening! You won't believe it. We called James's lawyer, and he had a copy of the will. I am the sole beneficiary now, I mean now that Jason is gone, and can you believe it? I'm going to inherit forty-two million dollars. Forty-two million."

I smiled. "You deserve it, after what he put you through."

"Oh, and guess what? Ronald and I are putting the big house on the market. I had too many nightmares there to be able to move back. Ronald's mom has lived here for fifty-six years, so this is her home and we can't move her now. And we are all happy here. And I talked to Dana Burke. She's so nice. I'm giving the Mourned Miners ten million dollars."

Her childlike excitement was heartwarming and made me happy. I tried to picture Dana's reaction to that news and smiled again. "That's fantastic."

"We are going to run the Mourned Miners together. We are going to try to take it national. It's going to feel so good using James's money for something good. Something helpful."

"I came out to let you know that Marcus Freedman and his wife, Betty Ann—they were Tameka's parents—are interested in adopting Maddie. Do you have any objection to that?"

Patricia thought for a long minute. "I don't. I don't want to raise any more kids, and I'm sure they are going to take good care of her. Can I meet her?"

"I'm sure that can be arranged. We can go from there."

"One more piece of news," Ronald said, smiling at her. He nodded at her left hand, which he was holding gently.

"Oh! Oh, yes! We are getting married!"

That brought a huge smile to my face. "Wow! Congratulations!" I fawned over the antique ring, a beautiful square diamond set into an intricate fourteen-karat gold band.

"It was his mother's. I love it. And her. I'm so happy. Is that wrong?"

"Not at all."

"I'll send you an invitation to the wedding, to DHS."

"I can't wait to see it." I stood up and gathered my purse and handed her a business card with the address on it. "I'll be in touch in about a week, after I meet with the Freedmans, and we'll arrange for you to meet your granddaughter."

When I got back to the office, I was summoned to Mac's office. He motioned for me to take a seat in the chair in front of his desk.

"How are you?"

"Fine."

"Try again. Any nightmares?"

"I haven't had any so far. Did absolutely nothing yesterday."

"Good. You needed a break. How's LaReesa?"

"She's fine. Wants to graduate and go to cosmetology school. She's catching up."

"Tell me about this friendship with Kirk Mahoney."

I shrugged. "It's just that. A friendship. He asks me for information on my cases, which I don't ever give him. Sometimes he helps me. He was actually the one who found James Alsbrook, after we took Maddie Freedman into custody."

I updated Mac about all my other cases, and he said he was taking me off the new investigation rotation for a few days. I appreciated his having my back.

I did updates for the rest of the afternoon and picked Reese up at school, on time, which got no comment. I pulled into the carport and Reese went down to the mailbox to fetch the mail. When she returned, she held a handful of junk mail and one white envelope. I held out my hand, expecting a bill.

"It's fo' me."

"Oh, okay then."

We went into the house and stood in the living room as she tore open the envelope. I watched as her expression went from curious, to interested, to concerned.

"What's up?" I asked.

"This letter from my mamma." She read on, silently, and then said, "She gettin' out, March first."

Chapter Twenty Five

LaReesa continued, "Ms. Vanessa let her know where I was, and gave her dis address."

"That's okay."

She read on. "She want me to come live with her when she get out. I don't have to, do I? She say she gonna get clean and get a job. But she ain't."

I could see and feel her anxiety rising. She spoke quickly and her voice rose. "She done said that before so many times and she never do. I wanna stay here. I got a good school and some friends. I don't wanna go with her!"

I walked over to her and took her hands. "Look at me. Listen to me. Take a deep breath." I waited while that happened. "It is not up to your mama where you live. You are in the custody of the State of Alabama. You cannot go live with her until the judge says you can."

I waited while the relief from that realization flooded her face. "Really?"

"Really. If she wants custody of you, she is going to have to prove to Family Court that she can take care of you. By getting housing. Working, doing something legal. She is going to have to get a job, and keep it, and pass drug tests for the court. And prove that for a few months before she can even think about getting you back. Plus, after she does all that, the judge will listen to you and where you want to be. The best thing you can do is prove to him that this is good place for you. That you are staying in school, improving your grades, staying out of trouble, and doing well here."

"And you don't mind if I stay here?"

"Of course not, especially if you do well."

She threw her arms around my neck in an impulsive hug, which I returned.

"Can I go write her a letter and tell her all that?" she asked.

"How about you do homework first? Then write your mom? It'll give you a chance to calm down, and think about what you want to say."

She handed me the letter from her mother. I glanced at it while she gathered her bookbag and headed for the dining room. The return address was Julia Tutwiler Prison, Highway 231 in Wetumpka, Alabama. Her mother's handwriting was childlike, the letter looked like it had been written by a fourth grader. It stated everything LaReesa had said, and ended with a paragraph stating she loved her so much and missed her so much and had a lot of hearts drawn on it.

Reese reluctantly settled with her books, complaining about Science as she filled out a worksheet. I sat across from her at the table, working on my laptop as she did homework. She finished her homework and retrieved a blank notebook page to write her mother. She wrote for a while, and when she was finished, she passed the notebook to me.

"What do you think?" she asked. I took the notebook. Her handwriting was a small, neat cursive. I read,

Dear Mamma,

I got your letter. I live with Ms. Claire now. She real nice. She a social worker. We live in Hoover and I go to a good school. I like it here. Ms. Claire say if you want me to live with you, you got to do a few things. You got to stay off drugs and you got to get a house. You got to get a job to get money. Then the judge has to say ok.

I hope you can do what you want. I hope you can stay off drugs. Good luck.

Love,
LaReesa Jones

I found an envelope for Reese and, as she was addressing it, Grant got home early and found us there. He was carrying something in from the carport.

I saved my work on my laptop and looked up. Boxes. He was carrying boxes. He took them back the office. When I followed him back there, he was putting them together with a roll of packing tape.

"What's going on?"

"I'm moving out."

"What? Why?"

"You know why."

"Because of LaReesa?"

"No."

"Grant—I don't—what—" I thought I did know, and wondered how he found out.

"You are cheating on me."

I can't lie. I never have been able to, and get away with it. Instead of denying it, I said, "What makes you think that?"

He pulled out his phone and pulled up his pictures. He showed me the first one, which was one of Kirk, kissing me on the cheek. The second was me touching Kirk's face. There was a look of tenderness and caring on my face that made me wince.

I said, "You followed me?"

"You have been treating me like a roommate for a month now. Or a babysitter. It was clear you were no longer interested in this relationship, and I wanted to find out why. Now I know. It's clear you are not ready for something long term. So, I'm out."

"I don't want you to go."

"Too bad. So you did sleep with him."

I looked down at the floor as my eyes filled with tears. "Once," I whispered. "That picture you took was the day I was saying goodbye to him. I wanted to work on us."

"Too late."

He packed all his computers into the boxes, then he folded the trestle tables and loaded all of that into his van. Then went into our bedroom, where he threw his clothes from the closet and the dresser into another box.

LaReesa and I watched in the driveway as he loaded those boxes. He approached us and took out his keys. He took the house key off his ring and handed it to me. "Bye," he said.

"Bye," I whispered.

LaReesa was choking back tears.

We watched as his van cranked and left, rounding the curve in the road.

LaReesa came and stood beside me, tears on her face. She placed her hand in mine.

"Did he leave cause of me? Is dis my fault?"

"No, honey. It's all mine."

Other books in the
Social worker Claire Conover Mystery Series

Little Lamb Lost

Social worker Claire Conover honestly believed she could make a difference in the world until she got the phone call she's dreaded her entire career. One of her young clients, Michael, has been found dead, and his mother, Ashley, has been arrested for his murder. And who made the decision to return Michael to Ashley? Claire Conover.

Ashley had seemingly done everything right - gotten clean, found a place to live, worked two jobs, and earned back custody of her son. Devastated but determined to discover where her instincts failed her, Claire vows to find the truth about what really happened to Michael.

What Claire finds is no shortage of suspects. Ashley's boyfriend made no secret that he didn't want children. And Ashley's stepfather, an alcoholic and a chronic gambler, has a shady past. And what about Michael's mysterious father and his family? Or Ashley herself? Was she really using again?

Amidst a heap of unanswered questions, one thing is for certain: Claire Conover is about to uncover secrets that could ruin lives - or end her own.

**ature*Little Girl Gone*

Claire Conover is back in the sequel to *Little Lamb Lost*. She has taken a 13-year-old girl into custody after she is found sleeping behind a grocery store. The girl's murdered mother is found at a construction site owned by a family friend, then the girl disappears. Her mother worked in an illegal gambling industry in Birmingham. Things only get more complicated from there. Is it possible the girl pulled the trigger? She doesn't have a lot of street smarts, so where could she have run? Claire has to find the answers, and the girl, fast.

CPSIA information can be obtained
at www.ICGtesting.com
Printed in the USA
BVHW091521020123
655321BV00013B/685